Listen T
Your
Heartbeats

By the same author

Tinkling of the Bell... Before it Rings

When Jai met Sakshi, by sheer chance, he couldn't have imagined he'd one day be visiting Europe with her for a countryside fashion tour. All he heard was the tinkling of a bell somewhere in his heart.

When Sakshi met Jai the next time, she barely knew their friendship would run deeper than anything she had ever wished for.

He is an aspiring police officer and she wants to be a leading designer in the world of fashion. Will their different paths take them to the same destination we call love, or will hurdles change the way love happens?

More than that, is love really enough? Join their journey as they find out in the *Tinkling of the Bell... Before it Rings.*

Listen To Your Heartbeats

SONIKA SHANDILYA

Srishti
PUBLISHERS & DISTRIBUTORS

Srishti Publishers & Distributors
Registered Office: N-16, C.R. Park
New Delhi – 110 019
Corporate Office: 212A, Peacock Lane
Shahpur Jat, New Delhi – 110 049
editorial@srishtipublishers.com

First published by
Srishti Publishers & Distributors in 2020

10 9 8 7 6 5 4 3 2 1

Printed and bound in India

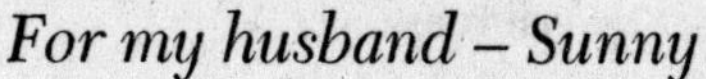

For my husband – Sunny

Acknowledgment

My parents' and brother's love makes me go about doing things, and this book is one of them.

My in-laws, who have loved me the way I am, and gave me the confidence to write.

Manisha, I want to tell you that your patience in listening to the manuscript has seen me through the book.

My sons Suryaab and Shwetab's interest in whatever I do. Their appreciation made me an author even before my books were published.

1

The lights at the Amer Fort in Jaipur were kissing it at various places, yet not getting enough. It made the lights even hungrier. But there was one person hungrier than the lights – Sonam. Sonam was sitting in one of the chairs, watching the light and sound show. The sound of *ghungroos* through speakers met the sound of Sonam's payal resting on her ankle, with small diamond shaped plates of silver joined with delicate dots. The sound of ghungroos came in layers – an elaborate announcement of arrival of the princess. She wore a knee-length frock with big flowers in different shades of lilac. The delicacy of the lilac flowers flowed in the chiffon fabric of the frock.

The lights became bright now, illuminating the audience. Sonam tapped her foot hard on the ground, enjoying the sound of her payal mingle with the sound of ghungroos spilling out of the huge speakers. Sonam hid her payal by pulling her scarf, as she tapped. Not that she cared what other people thought, but she didn't want these modern people to come in her world of kings, queens, princesses and princes. The lights swept back to the royalty, while other beams of light took Sonam along. Sonam felt the small white pearls of the nose ring on her lips, taking along a bit of lipstick. Sonam adjusted her back straight in the plastic chair, feeling herself in the royal courtyard of Amer Palace. Her hair was being blown with the wind, while her elaborate ghagra and dupatta did justice to her payal and royal spirits.

Just behind the area where Sonam sat, stood a small hillock, watching the fort, admiring its beauty in different shades of sunlight and moonlight. But Rann Vijay Rathore was not interested in watching the Amer fort in any shade. He sat atop the hillock, leaning his back against a tree, resting his arm on a wooden barrel-shaped ice-box. He finished the last sip of his whiskey in one go. He poured another peg of Chivas Regal crossing the limit of Patiala Peg. He dropped five cubes of ice in his whisky. The sound of ice cubes colliding against each other said cheers to Rann Vijay.

"Cheers!" replied Rann Vijay and lifted the glass before taking a big sip of the drink, feeling the tingling sensation in his mouth and something went galloping to his head. "It is difficult to decide whether I enjoy beer more or whisky," said Rann Vijay to himself, shaking his glass to hear the tinkling of the ice-cubes, his only companions of the day. His broad shoulders rested nicely on a thick tree trunk. In dark blue jeans and Black Light denim shirt, he sat on the ground sheet, which did not accommodate his feet, owing to his six feet-two inches frame. RV's (Rann Vijay's) fair complexion made his beard reflect green, even though it was nicely shaved. His hair was well trimmed; neither too short, nor too long, just enough to give him a royal look.

RV lifted his chin and forced his eyes to open, which were being pushed close by the pegs he had downed. His hazel eyes were enough to fill many bottles of Chivas Regal. There was one more thing shutting RV's eyes – the moon. The full moon directly looked into them, worried about its *chandni* falling for his brown eyes.

RV's thick eyelashes stood like a guard, fencing the sleeping eyes. RV's closed eyes lay like an antique beautiful box, which had everyone yearning to see what was inside the box. The moon's chandni spread everywhere, being more partial to the closed eyes.

Sonam sat at the Jharokha, enjoying the attention given by the lights of the show. The dance of the lights finally stopped and plain white light took over. The show ended and Sonam realized that she was sitting on a boring plastic chair, all the while dreaming about being the princess of this amazing palace.

"Oh god, I want to see this show again," Sonam desperately wanted the Amer Fort to show its grandeur in these lights once again. Sonam got up thinking why would god have time for such silly wishes.

"The Hindi version of the show will start in another ten minutes," the person in-charge announced.

"God does listen!" She settled back in her chair for putting on another royal dress and jewellery to skim through the magnificent fort.

Something made her look up. She wanted to check if such a strong white light came from the moon. She saw just an arched outline of the moon behind the hillock. Sonam looked back two or three times to see the full moon emerging out and above the hillock.

The second show also ended after a while, but Sonam was glued to the seat. All the visitors left, leaving Sonam in a magical stupor.

"Hello madam, there is no show after this," the caretaker's voice shook her back to reality.

"Oh!" was all she could say, as she walked back to her taxi.

Her hair fell in layers, with the front layer falling a little below her chin. The layer of her hair which fell till the waist swayed a little, enjoying the soft *chhum chhum* of her anklets.

"Wait! Wait ma'am." She stopped as she saw the palace chowkidar come running.

"Ma'am, RV sir has slept under a tree on this hillock. He had a little too much to drink. He is alone today. He comes here often, not always to drink." He said sheepishly, "Can you please drop him to his house? His driver is not picking up the phone," the chowkidar went on as Sonam looked up and saw a silhouette of a man.

"Ok! I will also climb up to see what has happened to him." Sonam saw this as an excuse to climb the hillock. She adjusted the scarf with two rounds around her neck to make it more convenient to climb. Sonam enjoyed the breeze over her sleeveless dress as she climbed, admiring the moonlit Amer fort and slowing down occasionally to look at the Maota Lake. She spotted RV under the tree from far. After walking a little towards RV, she stopped and could not move.

'Have the lights scooped out a prince out of Amer Palace and left him here? He looks like some prince who came travelling from a far off land and slept here for a while before resuming his journey,' Sonam thought.

'The royal spirits of the Amer Palace have been very kind to me today,' thought Sonam as she admired this prince under the tree.

"Ma'am, we will need one more person to bring him down."

"I will call the taxi driver. Oh! There he comes." The taxi driver had also followed them there to be a part of this adventure. With each arm resting on the shoulder of the watchman and the taxi driver, RV came down and they made him sit in the front seat of the taxi.

The watchman showed his concern and told the driver the way to RV's bungalow. Sonam sat right behind the driver's seat. As Rann Vijay lay peacefully in his reclined seat, Sonam felt royalty was sitting next to her. And this is what she enjoyed the most – feeling royal.

The concern of the watchman like a true loyal of the king hinted at Rann Vijay Rathore being some royal prince. 'This watchman is so concerned for this prince,' thought Sonam as she adjusted in her seat to be at a position most convenient for her to look at the prince. 'The watchman said his name is RV. What could it stand for? Some long name fit for a prince.' While her brain indulged in mental dialogue, her eyes were busy appreciating RV's looks. Just like an artist would appreciate art, a nature photographer would feast his lens on hues of sky, colourful birds. 'Attraction is not essential to admire beauty. Having such a tall neck, broad shoulders, cheeks with highness and glamour of throne, the skin shining like gems of a crown – is qualification enough to be a prince.' Sonam's mind was busy finding royal connections for RV. 'His eyes are the special treasure box in the treasury, which would be keeping armies across borders busy planning invasion.'

The taxi driver was a local chap and the way had been well explained by the palace watchman, so he did not disturb Sonam and her tryst with the prince.

The car light fell on a board which read "Rathore Bungalow" on the pillar that supported an elaborate big black iron gate, which had a stamp of royalty in golden paint on certain intricate designs.

The guard at the gate came out to ask who was there. "Oh! Chhote saab, what happened?" The man's face turned grim, which spoke of his concern.

"Nothing, he is drunk," the taxi driver said, trying to wipe his grin.

"Oh no! Chhote saab insisted he wanted to go alone today. Get the car inside, I will inform Bhagwant Singh," the guard said.

The well-maintained huge gate opened without any creaky sound. It opened to a driveway lined with antique lamps perched on top of about five feet high poles. Each of them broke into two halves making a W, each displaying their lamps. While Sonam was appreciating the lamps, they followed a curved path across a lush green fence which enclosed a big garden perhaps. Yes, it did. Now that the taxi had stopped at the porch, Sonam could see the lawn. To her left was the entrance of the house and to her right was the entrance to a big circular lawn and the road in between. All kinds of garden lights invited her inside.

Bhagwant Singh was more tense than the watchman and he kept calling, "RV Baba.."

Another aged helper emerged from the house to take RV inside. "Ma'am, please be seated in the drawing room, I will get coffee," the man helping Bhagwant Singh told Sonam.

"It's okay. It's getting late, I will go now. You take care of him," Sonam replied.

It was eleven' O clock. As her taxi rode on the other curved palm of the driveway, Sonam only thought of lifting the cover of the treasure box – RV's eyes, to see what was inside those eye lids.

Sonam reached Hotel Marriott and instructed the driver, "Come at ten tomorrow morning," and headed for dinner at the restaurant.

She walked down the corridor and took left for the restaurant. There were a few people and the buffet looked bored, being there since seven thirty. Sonam picked up a plate and without much thought picked up some vegetarian stuff. She sat on a table near the window, deliberately avoiding the dimly lit table at the corner. She did not like anything which was held back and boring.

2

When Sonam opened her eyes in her comfortable hotel bed, the soft shade lit the otherwise dark room and did not give away what time it was.

She picked her cellphone, unplugging the charger to see the time. "Oh! 9 a.m.!"

She drew the dark curtains to look out of the glass. "This is amazing," was all she could say, yearning to come closer to the open arms of Jaipur spread as far as she could see."

She sat in the taxi with a tangy aftertaste of orange juice she had for breakfast. "Madam, where do you want to go today," asked the taxi driver.

She looked out of the window, thought for a while and said "City Palace". Sonam did not like the structural slavery of an itinerary; she did what she felt like. Her pink lipstick just added a little more pink and shine to flaunt her cupid's bow and tear drop earrings. As the Innova stopped in front of the City Palace gate, she stepped out in classy cotton ankle length skirt with silver chains tied at the waist. With her hair covering the thin strips of her white tank top, she breezed inside.

This was the first monument she saw during the day as she had landed only the previous afternoon. "This is magic," she said a little loudly, slowly raising her neck, moving her eyes over the rising palace till her neck could no longer go backward. 'The pink meets the blue,' Sonam admired the palace against the sky with her eyes skimming the delicate carving. It was like the palace was teeming with magic and Sonam breezed in to live that era. She slipped into the royal costumes to say hello to the princess that she was.

After two hours, she came out to walk on the streets with silver shops, colourful puppets, bandhani clothes, and all other shops that made the streets vibrantly alive. She felt part of the celebration that the old era at the City Palace had spilled out to the streets. She went inside an antique silver shop and picked up an antique elaborate neck piece with a hint of delicacy.

"Ma'am this is an antique piece," the shopkeeper spoke in English with accent, thinking that she was some pretty foreigner.

"*Bhaiya, yeh kitne ka hai*?" Sonam deliberately asked in Hindi, trying to tell the shopkeeper that Indians are prettier than foreigners. Sonam admired the choker against her tall neck in a mirror, but did not buy anything, since she wanted to explore the other shops too.

"Bhaïya, which is the best shop for blue pottery," she asked someone. She soon reached the pottery shop and saw different vases. But Sonam was not enjoying herself as RV's closed eyes still tugged at her heart.

"What is wrong with me?" she questioned herself. "I don't even know his full name. What if he is involved with some girl? No! No god, no! Please, he should not have any girlfriend."

Sonam was standing and looking at blue pottery when the shopkeeper interrupted. "Ma'am, do you want to see how the pottery is made? I can show."

"No, I have to go now," she came out to get in the car, not sure where she should go.

"Ma'am where do you want to go?" the driver asked when she did not say anything.

"Switch on the A.C., I will just sit here for a while," she said, sliding a little to rest her head on the seat. Sonam's smooth and fair complexion, her amber eyes, nose which competed with her eyes in beauty, the down slope from her chin, all tried to shoo the thoughts away from her face. Even bad thoughts did not have the heart to tread her beauty away.

'Am I mad? No, I must be mad if I don't meet RV again!' She straightened herself as she planned it out in her mind. She called the driver and said, "Bhaiya, you remember we left someone at his house yesterday?"

"Of course ma'am, we climbed to get him. How can I forget?"

"Okay, let's go there then," Sonam said.

'What will I say? I have come to see how RV was?' The car ran on the road as the thoughts of how exciting it will be to meet RV ran in her mind. Sonam's amber eyes shone brighter and a smile hopped from her lips to her cheeks, as she imagined RV with his eyes open. As they approached the gate of RV's house, she saw a peacock on one of the pillars. Sonam felt a flutter in her heart. The fanning of feathers caused more than a flutter, but before Sonam could break into her own version of peacock dance, she felt a certain stage fright.

"Bhaiya, don't turn. Please keep going straight," Sonam told the driver. With a blank mind, she kept going on the road for fifteen minutes when she saw a super market.

"Bhaiya, stop in front of this supermarket."

Sonam walked in to the supermarket. The bright sun rays of the afternoon fell on her voluminous brown hair, making them blush golden.

When she entered the shop, her eyes caught hold of chilled almond milk. Her throat was dry, because of many reasons.

"Bhaiya, *khol ke de do*," she told the shop keeper.

She took the open bottle to gulp, when she heard, "Hukum, this is *sharab*. I don't drink."

"No, Bhagwant Singh, this is not sharab; this is only a cold drink." Sonam was taking a gulp from the bottle when she heard this and turned to look. What she saw, made her gulp. She saw RV with the person who had helped him go inside the house yesterday. Sonam's five feet six inches height made sure that she did not waste time lifting her eyes to look into the eyes of this tall guy. She just sank into them with no desire to swim back. His drop dead good looks were her oxygen. What she did not realize was that she was not sinking alone; RV was also with her, with no desire to reach the bottom or to come up to the surface.

'Was she some princess whose beauty was not contained in history and had come in this modern age to visit her palace?" RV did not think, but felt, as his ability to think had been robbed by her beauty. Two more things got robbed – their hearts. Heart is the only thing in the world which feels beautiful when lost.

"Hukum, I have got this Appy Fizz." Bhagwant Singh came with a bottle in his hand, and some nachos.

He saw Sonam and said, "Hukum, she is the one who brought you home yesterday."

When RV heard this, the bottle of cold drink almost slipped off his hand. This time a thought came to his mind. 'The best thing about whiskey – such a gorgeous girl comes with you in the car.' The bad thing about whiskey – you don't remember it.

"Ma'am, you went without having coffee," Bhagwant Singh said as he walked towards her, armed with all kinds of eatables.

RV tried to cut a few threads of the net of her enigma he found himself caught in. He went up to her and said, "Hi! I am Rann Vijay Rathore." He extended his hand.

"Hi RV," she said, meeting his hand for a hand shake, feeling pleased with her decision to come to this supermarket.

"So you know I am RV."

"Yes, you are popular at the Amber Fort."

She smiled and continued, "I am Sonam. Sonam Singh."

'Sonam, you are popular with all the royalty and beauty across the world.' This is what he said in his mind, but something else out loud, "Sonam, it's great to meet you. You heard my popularity for all the wrong reasons, I am afraid."

They shook hands, both unsure if it was for real. "Not at all, Rann Vijay Rathod. It was like some loyal sewaks of the royals concerned for their prince."

"Why don't you come home with us? We need to thank you properly and there is a special occasion today. It is Bhagwant Singh's birthday. In fact, we are here to shop for the party." RV looked adorable inviting Sonam, as he stood wearing light blue ripped jeans with a light orange plain T-shirt. The light denim jacket with some streaks of silver, which almost blended with the faded blue made RV look just one of his kind.

"Janam din bahut bahut mubarak ho aap ko," Sonam wished Bhagwant Singh.

"Aase nahi, ghar chaliye," Bagwant Singh invited her to come to their house sincerely, hoping she agreed.

"Don't worry Sonam, I have only cold drink here," RV showed her the bottle.

"I didn't worry yesterday also."

Now apart from the looks, RV loved her prompt and interesting reply also. "Let's go then," RV said.

"My taxi is right here," Sonam told him as she kept her half full bottle of chilled milk aside.

"Let me take the pleasure of driving you home in my car today," RV said smiling. "Bhagwant Singh, get ten bottles of chilled Almond milk too and get her taxi home," RV told Bhagwant Singh.

Sonam instructed her taxi driver to come with Bhagwant Singh, before walking towards RV's Audi 05.

"Please," RV said as he opened the door of the royal blue Audi. "You are visiting Jaipur?" RV asked Sonam as he turned the SUV to the right.

"Yes," Sonam replied, realizing that it was much more fun sitting on the seat next to RV and with him in full senses. Rann Vijay wanted to tell her why he was drunk the previous evening, but he didn't want to spoil the good vibes of the ride with Sonam.

"Wow RV! I could not see the fields your house is surrounded with when I came last night. Stop here, please. I want to go run in these fields."

"Let's reach the porch," RV said. We can go from there."

"No, I want to go now. Can't wait," Sonam replied.

"Okay." RV was amused at her thrill and stopped the car. By the time RV put off the ignition, Sonam had already crossed the flower beds which lined the road and was trying to run on dry lumps of hard mud. RV did not want to waste time coming out of the car, he just watched Sonam approaching the golden wheat which reflected the reddish blush of the sun as the rays got involved with the evening. Sonam now walked in the water channel lightly brushing the crop with her hands. At times she would stand and just gaze at the vast field of wheat which ran along with the sky and finally embraced it.

Sonam cupped her hands to shout "RV, come!" as RV still sat twisted in the driver's seat, looking at her from the car's window.

"I will," RV called back and started walking swiftly towards her. The flirtatious evening rays of the sun entered RV's hazel eyes, charming the predominant brown in them. There was a huge Neem tree growing at the far end of the field. The month of April had dressed the tree in a few leaves and as Sonam stood there admiring the whole place, her eyes fell on a huge peacock on the tree. Her eyes moved from his crown and slipped over his bluish green shiny neck on to the long tail full of feathers. As the peacock walked gracefully on the thick branch of the tree, she felt a lovely feeling treading her heart.

"Sonam," called RV, but did not complete his sentence as he saw Sonam put a finger on her lips, pointing towards the peacock. His shoulders lightly brushed hers' as he tried to see what she was showing. 'Peacocks are as common as blue pottery in Jaipur,' RV wanted to say, but did not, looking at her enthusiasm. The peacock just flew and when she turned to look at RV, she planted a nice big kiss on his cheek. When one sees a face that redefines good looks, what can a person do? The golden hue of the ripe wheat and the orangish yellow sunlight mixed together to conspire for this kiss. When the rays came out of RV's eyes, they were intoxicated. They raised a toast to his ruffled hair simmering in brown and gold.

Before RV could decide whether to get stunned or just enjoy the moment, Sonam said, "Don't read anything in this kiss. This is what I would give to any beautiful flower, jewellery or peacock.

"But Sonam, my name comes in your list of things you can kiss," RV said with a smile dancing on his lips, risking another kiss.

"RV, I don't analyze too much. I do what I feel like, and don't regret," Sonam replied. RV didn't want to say anything about the kiss further, as he felt his heart warm up to Sonam's innocent implusive nature.

"Okay then, let's go and celebrate Bhagwant Singh's birthday." RV started walking with her to the bungalow with a strong urge to ask her if he was the first guy who triggered her impulse, but suppressed it. They entered a round lawn in front of the porch, where she had seen various lights glitter last night.

Bhagwant Singh, along with an elderly person and a middle-aged lady were busy laying tables, chairs and putting some balloons to set up a small birthday party.

"Jayanti, get glasses from inside," the elderly helper called out when he saw RV and Sonam enter. "*Khamma ghani* madam,

Bahut khushi hui aap se mil kar. Aap ka dhanyawad Karna tha." The old man said and his face lit up when he saw Sonam.

"Sonam, he is Roop Singh ji. He is with me from the time I was born. He is my guru," RV said with affection.

"Kya hukum," Roop singh said with love and respect.

"Roop Singh ji, don't call me hukum. I am like your son."

"Sonam ji, why did you go without coffee yesterday," Roop Singh asked as she was still thinking about RV's affectionate nature.

"Roop singh ji, I will have it today," Sonam replied.

"Give some juice to Sonam's driver also," RV called out as he walked with Sonam, seeing the colourful flower beds.

"What are these flowers called?" Sonam asked pointing out to the riot of colours outside the circular lawn at the far end of the porch.

"Those are sweet peas. We will go around the house before it gets dark," RV said as he walked with Sonam, leaving everyone else in the lawn, working for the party. Delicate sweet peas stood playfully over a wine with tendrils winding over the light bamboo support. Sonam felt the softness of a petal between her fingers. The innocence of the flower, the shine, softness, colours of all possible shades, sweet lingering smell could all be captioned "First love". RV was also discovering the beauty of the sweet peas in his house for the first time. Just then, Sonam saw something very shiny, almost inside the flowers.

'Sunbird!' She slowly moved her hands as the word vibrated in her mind. Before RV could realize, the bird was in her hand. "Look at this RV, I caught it," she showed the delicate bird, which looked quite safe in her beautiful hands. She almost ran to the lawn to show everyone the same. RV felt a flutter of zing in his house.

"We used to play catching this bird when chhote hukum was a kid. Hukum *bhi pakar kar hifazat se chhor dete the*," Roop Singh said.

"*Phikar mat kijiye bhaiya*, we will also give her freedom." She said something softly, bringing the bird close to her lips, and then extended her hands to let go of the bird. RV and everyone else looked at the bird as she shimmerred in its shiny blues and greens and the love she got from Sonam.

3

"Bhagwant Singh ji, do you feel drunk?" RV asked as he adjusted a few cushions on the ground to lean on his elbow and to make himself comfortable on the grass. Sonam also understood that they would not be sitting on in the chairs, so she also sat on the grass, resting her back on one of the sofas.

"Bahut nasha hua hukum," Bagwant singh replied.

"What Bhagwant Singh ji? Just from a wine bottle lookalike?" RV said.

"Nahi aap ke pyar our izzat se." The love and respect you give to us is so genuine, hukum.

"What are you saying Bhagwant Singh ji! I have spent my childhood with you all, listening to stories and playing. Roop Singh ji, Sonam has come to Rajasthan for the first time. Why don't you tell her a Rajasthani story."

"Koi lok katha, anything you like," Sonam said, grabbing the opportunity to fulfil her childhood wish to listen to stories late in the night.

Roop Singh and Jayanti sat cross legged. "Camel cart moved up and down, while the camel enjoyed pounding his hoofs up and down the desert." Roop Singh started with the story in a mix of Hindi and Rajasthani accent. "A young princess was sitting inside her palace. Her lover, a farmer, drove the camel cart and was fast approaching the palace. When the cart came close to the vast deserts of Pushkar, he called out, 'Rani Sa, come join me!'" The story went on as RV and Sonam got more and more engrossed in it. Bhagwant Singh and Jayanti could see the cart on the Pushkar desert. The soothing rhythm of the story and the perfect narration by Roop Singh walked its way into a yawn of Sonam. Sonam's dreamy eyes were drunk with their own beauty and when RV saw this, his eyes got entangled in her tipsy eyes and refused to blink. The caressing by the story, the cool still starry night with cool breeze of RV's personality blowing, filled Sonam's head with the sweetness of sleep. Sonam crawled closer to the sofa and rested her head on her arm over the cushion. The story ended on a happy note and RV slowly withdrew his eyelashes from Sonam's eyes, which were closed now.

"Sonam, why don't you sleep here only instead of going back to the hotel?" RV said.

Sonam made an effort to lift her eyes to reply, "I had not thought anything about sleep. I was just enjoying the story."

"Sonam ji, I can put adventure tents here in the ground for you and hukum," Bhagwant singh said.

"Yes Sonam, we will put tents for all five of us like some adventure camp. It will be much more fun than your hotel room." RV wanted everyone's tent there, so that Sonam felt more secure and it did feel like an adventure!

The mere idea of sleeping in a beautiful lawn under the stars made her say yes. Within a few minutes, the circular lawn turned into a camping site with tents being pegged inside, with everyone working together like a team.

RV was going inside to get some water when he saw Sonam's driver, "Bhai, what is your name?"

"I am Jaswant Singh, hukum."

"Okay Jaswant Singh, would you like to sleep in the tent or you want to go home?"

"Hukum, I will be happy to sleep in the tent, if you permit."

"Bhagwant Singh, put one tent for Jaswant also," RV called out as he went inside the house. Sonam admired her tent, looking at the netted top, which would be her passport to travel to the stars.

"Where are you lost, Sonam?" RV asked, passing her a bottle of cold water.

"I don't get to enjoy all this in Delhi," she said before taking a sip of water.

"Out on a solo trip?" RV Questioned.

"Yeah!" Sonam said as she took a little longer to gulp water, as if trying to gulp something else too. "After my last exam of third year college, I just packed up some stuff and came to Jaipur. I had landed that afternoon only when I saw you at Amber Fort."

"I know you do things on an impulse," RV said rubbing his fingers on his cheek.

"Yes, I do RV, and I firmly believe that if you like to do something, you must go ahead without being trapped by ifs and buts. If I was not an impulsive person, I would not have agreed to stay here in a tent. I have met you for the first time, but I feel comfortable here, and safe. Sometimes people are not safe in their own homes."

"That is a big compliment for me."

"Yes, and the kiss was also a big compliment for you," Sonam smiled and entered her tent.

With so many compliments showered on him, how could he follow her in the tent, so he walked to his own. RV looked at the stars which appeared much brighter today and thought of the time when he last made himself act on an impulse.

He was falling asleep effortlessly. His house felt like home today. At six in the morning, the early summer sun looked like a *bindi* in all shades of reds and orange. This bindi was in love with the earth and she embraced it, coulouring it in the hues of orangish red. Sonam unzipped her tent and stepped outside on the green grass with fresh dew. RV was still asleep inside his tent.

"If we get hot tea in a tray, what more can one ask for." Sonam told Roop Singh when she saw him getting tea.

"Sonam ji, Jayanti is inside. We have put the essentials in the washroom. You can freshen up inside."

"That's great Roop Singh ji." She breezed inside the house. RV jumped out of his bed as if scared of the fact that Sonam could have left. He saw two empty cups yearning to be filled by the teapot sitting besides it. RV could identify himself with the situation of the cups. Just then he saw Sonam coming with her wet face, enjoying the breeze dry it.

"Good morning RV," Sonam settled on the chair with RV sitting next to him. "After the tea, I will leave," Sonam said pouring tea in cups.

"Sonam, no one can show you Jaipur better than me," RV told her.

'Yes, if your looks let me see anything else,' Sonam thought and said, "Come pick me up from the hotel in two hours."

"Bhaiya, I don't need the taxi now," she told the taxi driver when she reached Marriot. The enthusiasm of going with RV found her walking in the lobby, ready to go out just after an hour. Her light blue denim shorts could not have found a better waist to hug. Her white bishop-sleeved top flowed effortlessly and stayed just below the button of her shorts. Wearing race up sandals, she breezed out of the main door of the hotel.

As she stepped down the stairs, RV zoomed in his Audi and Sonam immediately went inside.

"How did you know I was coming," both said together and they laughed. RV didn't say but Sonam knew he was taking her to Amer Fort. This is what happens when people click. Sometimes people live for years together and never know what the other wants.

The dark blue waters of the lake turned green with envy when they saw RV and Sonam looking down at it.

"RV, the lake looks like a dark green emerald studded in a choker worn by this place."

"I never thought about the lake this way before," RV said admiring this piece of jewellery. "Come princess, to your palace," RV gestured with his hand as they entered the huge gate. Today, Sonam did not need any aid of payal or imagination to feel like a princess. Just his presence was enough to make her feel like a princess. They breezed from one part of the fort to another, not living that era, but creating their own. The era of the fort did provide background music for Sonam and RV, though. This was not any instrumental soft music, but electric guitar, maraca, Drums, Cowbells – which made their heart and soul break into hip-hop street dancing and Latin moves.

They were at the top layer of the fort when the sun greeted them with a hot flying kiss, it being at its prime at one in the afternoon. Both of them turned towards a downward pathway cut out of big rocks.

RV's ripped light blue jeans also got into the groove when RV hit the side of his thigh twice to synchronize the steps of his heart. Then his left arm rose in response to a step of his heart. Sonam also partnered, with her heart celebrating its happiness. It was all happening in their heart and mind only. They left their heart to be each other's partner now. Sonam and RV's eyes picked up each other's smile, celebrating this new partnership. Sonam extended her right foot diagonally with her left foot landing behind the right on its toes. RV also moved similarly, as they crisscrossed, their eyes never leaving each other. There were a very few people on this side of the fort and no one passed through RV and Sonam's way.

After about 5-6 crisscross steps, they jumped on their left foot while their right hand went up and they screamed, "Yeah!"

"Sonam, I have never met anyone who is so much fun."

"I have before, at the Amer Fort." RV's smile slipped when Sonam continued to tell him what all had happened at night on top of the hillock. RV's smile was able to climb back as it had not slipped too far.

They had reached near the souvenir shop of the fort. "RV, here take this glass, doesn't matter if it is day time." Sonam poured some imaginary wine from a turquoise decanter into two glasses. RV held the glass in one hand, while Sonam drank hers.

"Wait Sonam! How can you drink without cheers?"

"Sorry," said Sonam and clicked her glass with RV's.

The shop flowed into various corners of this elongated, not so claustrophobic cave. A salesman approached from a far corner. "Sir, ma'am, do you need any help?"

"Yes, can you get us some ice," Sonam said as she shook her glass lightly.

"What ma'am?" the salesman asks.

"I want ice to make our drink cold."

"She means a container for ice," RV said before the salesman labelled them insane.

"I will check in the other section."

As the salesman left, Sonam shook her glass while her eyes asked, "How should I drink without ice?

"Doesn't matter. Let's drink without ice."

"Okay then, bottoms up," said Sonam.

They both drank their imaginary drink and kept the glasses. Sonam looked at RV and said, "Didn't give any high. Let's try another one." Sonam poured another imaginary drink. Bottoms up and they ran out of the shop before the salesman could come back.

They stopped only when they reached the car. "I am actually feeling high now," RV said as he held the steering, resting his back against the seat.

"RV, I like to enjoy every moment to the fullest."

RV turned on the ignition, while thinking how these fun moments give a high and not his occasional drinking spree, which only gave him unconsciousness.

4

"Wait, wait! Stop here," Sonam said with enthusiasm in her voice.

"You want to learn how to make blue pottery!" RV said as he spotted the board 'Learn to make Blue pottery'. "We could have found something more interesting than this," RV said.

"RV, you might not have experienced the fun till now," she said as she opened the door and breezed inside.

"Can we learn how to make blue pottery?" Sonam asked the old man at the counter, whose face also required some polishing of the ceramic.

He led them to their workshop through the colourful blue pottery. In the centre was the potter's wheel which stood like a mother, proud of its various creations. The colour of the mud was pure, through which any dream could be created, and any colour of choice could be filled. Sonam quickly bent down and landed on her knees on the floor and tied her hair in a bun.

She started kneading the mixture. "Bhaiya, is this right?" innocently she kept asking for instructions as RV and her strands of hair got ruffled with her enthusiasm. Her pretty fingers had a nice coating of mud now which made them look like art in mud.

She suddenly rubbed her hands on RV's knees, giving them art in mud and said, "Sit now and knead this properly."

"No Sonam, I will go learn how to paint. It will help us when we set up our own workshop. I loved the art you made on my jeans. In fact, we can set a new trend – muddy tattered jeans." RV went to the corner where some workers were busy painting. RV took a brush, sat on the floor, smiled back at Sonam and started to paint.

Sonam brushed off the dust from her jeans before going to the car while RV let it stay. "Sonam, not a bad idea to start a workshop," RV said. "After I finished MBA, I have been thinking what to do."

"No RV, just doing this can be boring."

"No, this will be very exciting," RV teased. Sonam just smiled back in response.

"I have taken a few MBA entrance exams. Waiting for the results." Sonam said, as she stretched her legs to be more comfortable.

"Where did you do your MBA from?" Sonam asked.

"Harvard," RV answered.

"Oh! Foreign degree? But I want to do it from India."

"I also wanted to. But it is a symbol of prestige for my parents."

"I didn't meet your parents at your place." Sonam twisted in surprise.

"They are at Belgium right now. They travel eleven months in a year. We are into diamond business. They are busy expanding their business, exhibitions at different countries, selling to high profile customers." RV drove slow now, shifted a gear, struggling with his mood. Their car was circling a beautiful monument brought alive by the evening rays.

"What is this, RV?"

RV had not given it much thought, staying all these years in Jaipur, but Sonam's question scooped him out of his thoughts and his mind approached a full stop at the beauty of the building and his bubbly companion. "This is Albert Hall Museum. It is lighted up in the night too."

"Please RV, show me all the buildings which are lighted up at night."

Rann Vijay was wondering if people used the word 'please' if they were doing a favour to others. "We will drive towards Jaigarh Fort; it will be dark by then and will drive towards the city then."

"This sounds awesome," and she started to connect her phone's Bluetooth to the music system to rock the Audi with Latin American numbers. Sonam swayed her arms, taking the shoulders in a wave. RV hit these waves with the occasional claps which boomed in the car. They took two veg- burgers and French fries from a drive through McDonald's, not getting down from this rocking caravan. By the time they finished their burgers, the Audi had reached the Jaigarh Fort.

The soft yellow light which highlighted the fort had its own music of drums and electric guitar, which made Sonam plug out the music. They listened to the music created by the symphony of lights and the fort; of course the music direction and the lyrics were being given by Rann Vijay and Sonam. By the time they had driven along, seeing various forts and the city palace, both of them were an expert in lyrics and music direction.

"I want to write a song and sing in a music band – a very peppy number. The kind which will require an effort to sit and not dance, and still no one will succeed."

"What is the problem? You can join some band," RV said.

"The problem is I don't want that as a profession. I don't want an audience who would be sitting there to judge me on how I sing. And I don't want to just rehearse and then sing for money and then feel scared of losing my contracts because of ABC factors. I used to sing and play guitar for fun in school. Imagine RV, being in a band with a guitar in hand, no matter what and how the singing is. The whole experience will be so cool."

"Yes, the audience can be the trees and shrubs of the jungle."

"RV, this concert in a jungle will be so ..."

"Junglee!" RV completed the sentence.

"It will be wonderful if the lion comes to give a roaring applause." Sonam's excitement made her turn towards RV and her expression said she was already at the junglee concert.

RV pulled a face and said, "There are very less lions left in India, so chances of this roaring applause are very less."

Sonam burst into tears of laughter. Her eyes bared some of its depths like a clear sky after rain. RV just smiled, looked straight as he already had some plans and continued to drive.A message beeped on Sonam's phone, *"Do some meditation and sleep early."*

"I don't want to sleep." Sonam said loudly after putting her phone in the dash board.

She had not said this to RV, but RV replied, "Who wants to sleep? In fact, I was about to say, let's leave this car home and go for a drive on my bike. This is just a perfect time for the drive, empty roads, cool breeze."

"A mobike ride in the night! This is one of my dreams. There is so much traffic in Delhi and I never found any one to go with."

"I have gone many times, but always alone," RV said.

"No friends here?"

"They have all moved out following some trail or the other."

"And you did not follow any trail."

"I am just drifting, not looking for any trails."

"You are a great guy RV, good looks with brain."

RV gave an amused look to Sonam as he turned left and said, "My Harvard degree did not prove me intelligent?"

"No!" was her prompt answer.

RV's abrupt brake at the gate of his house spoke of his startled reaction. RV smiled at Sonam and said, "You are very intelligent."

"Yes and my intelligence says we should have something before we go for a ride."

"We will take packed dinner and have it on the way."

Breaking her routine from the normal time to sleep was a big adventure for Sonam. She just nodded, not able to believe what was happening in her life. 'Speeding on the bike late at night and whenever the moon beckons for a moon-lit dinner, we will agree.' Sonam was already on a bike in her thoughts, while still sitting in the Audi.

When RV came with his black Royal Enfield, Sonam opened the door and the *thuk thuk* sound of the bike synchronized with her heartbeat.

"Sonam, get something packed from Jayanti. Bhagwant Singh get an old cloth, we will clean this black beauty."

RV was already taking a round when Sonam came with two boxes of noodles and sandwiches. As RV adjusted the boxes in the front pocket, Sonam sat cross legged.

Sonam's hair band rested on her wrist while her hair enjoyed the freedom to fly in whichever direction they wanted to. Sonam held RV's shoulders, more for support than for any other reason.

"La la la la…" Sonam's right foot tapped on the foot rest and her head swayed while she sang this.

RV decreased his speed to hear if she was actually singing this cute childish song. RV thought about the kiss Sonam had given on his cheek. He was very sure now that the kiss was one of the cute little things about this pure hearted girl who would not keep anything in her heart.

'Has she stopped singing?' RV thought when he could hear only the sound of his bullet competing with the sound of the dark. "La la la la…" was the male voice provided by Rann Vijay.

Sonam enjoyed hearing this; it sounded more like the echo of her voice. The moon was determined to have a rocking night and it drummed silvery light everywhere. Sonam swayed to RV's song for a while, then she also joined in and both gave the most hit chorus.

Sonam cupped both her hands surrounding her lips and called out "Hoo hoo..." as she sat with RV on a machan in the midst of a ripe wheat field.

"What is this hoo hoo.. for?"

"Oh! That I was just trying to ward off anything that could be troubling the grains. And I wanted to get the feel of the machan too," she said turning to look at RV, who sat resting his head against the support of the bamboo while she sat letting her legs hang down. She took a bite of sandwich and said, "Rann Vijay, you deserve a prize for thinking of such a heavenly place for having dinner."

"You can always reward me with your appreciative kiss on the other cheek," RV said as a matter of fact as he dug his fork into noodles.

"Of course! I was waiting to finish this sandwich otherwise bread crumbs will stick to your cheek."

"Since when did you start thinking, Sonam?"

"Yes, I should not change my good habit." She got up and bent down to plant a nice noisy kiss on RV's left cheek, while transferring the bread crumbs too. The crumbs from the raw bread started to roast both on RV's cheek and Sonam's lips. This time, it did not stay an appreciative kiss.

She got up avoiding eye contact, back to her position of swaying legs. Now she swayed her legs just to convince herself that nothing had changed in this second kiss. She looked at the vast wheat field which was being guarded by the moon light. She was not able to convince herself that nothing had changed and she could not contain her excitement. She jumped down on the hay which lay on the ground.

'Yeah'! she said in her mind. RV's position with his back resting on the pole gave him a very clear view of her jump. The hay looked very cushy and before Sonam could call him, RV too jumped. After giving a little bounce, the hay adjusted under the curves of their backs. Rann Vijay and Sonam lay next to each other with a few hay stalks between them. It was a still, cool night so their gaze met the stars, their twinkling, which made the darkness look beautiful.

5

Sonam tossed in the bed of her hotel room. She was trying to get the comfort of the straw which had been so comfortable. Although she had come back late from the ride, still she could not get sound sleep. It was eight and she could no longer lie in bed. She got up and her soft cotton T-shirt also woke and stretched till the knee. Sonam looked out of the window, wondering if the sunshine could give her some brilliant idea – how to spend the day till evening when Rann Vijay came again. She was also wondering what important work RV had the whole day that he had told her he will come to the hotel only in the evening. She had come alone for a holiday and did not want to depend on someone she had just met for a good time, so she continued to look out. The morning sun rays were busy striking brown and golden hues on her hair and did not bother to give her any idea.

Sonam finally decided to get dressed and thought she would think how to spend her day while having her breakfast.

Delicate black lace hugged Sonam's neck and the chiffon fabric broke into uninhibited play of silver threads and the dress rejoiced in flair. "I will only enjoy the hotel today," Sonam found a good excuse to not go out.

There were many colourful shops at the Marriot. She picked up a bracelet which had an elephant trunk.

'I'll buy it,' she decided and pulled both the trunks and slid her wrist inside. Sonam admired her purchase as she paid the money. She got interested in a few batik printed skirts with silver stars scattered on them. She bought two of them in different colours. After this little shopping therapy, Sonam still didn't know what to do with her time.

"It is only afternoon now, and RV said evening. I wonder what time he will come. I will go and sit by the pool." She spotted a small bookshop there and picked a book from her favourite author – *Tinkling of the Bell... Before it Rings*. She made herself comfortable in one of the loungers, took a sip of fresh lime and started reading, 'I found a good way to spend time till RV comes,' thought Sonam, but she was wrong. She started getting restless after reading a few pages. She closed the book and walked around the pool.

Just then, a message beamed on her iPhone.

The message was from her father which said, '*We are going to an ashram near Yamunotri. Phones not allowed there. For something urgent you can contact us on 4647694659*'. Sonam read the message and pressed the home button hard to quickly make the message disappear from the screen and from her mind. She took out her headphones, attached them to her phone and listened to rocking music. The drums of this music helped her drum out any drab things. She walked around the pool as the music started producing little bubbles of zeal which had been hammered by the message.

Sonam took out her headphone and waved in excitement when she saw RV. Now so many bubbles were coming from RV that she found herself jumping to catch them. The thrill she missed even as a child and today she got even without the bubbles and actually jumping.

"Pack your bags. I have a big surprise for you," RV's eyes said the rest. "Meet Shiv, Veer and Aditi," RV said introducing the two young guys and a young lady. Sonam realized for the first time that RV had not come alone.

"And this has to be Sonam," Shiv, Veer and Aditi said together.

Even before Sonam could say hi, Shiv said, "Congrats, our band is ready. Give a high-five!" Sonam raised her hand for a high-five, while her eyes raised a confused look.

"Sonam, we will call our band the Surprise band," Veer said.

"It can be called Junglee too," Aditi said and jumped to give a high-five to Sonam. Sonam's hand was still up after the clap when she looked at RV with a twinkle in them. RV's eyes said it all. RV decided to put in words something which was hard to believe. But then there is something which makes things possible, which are sometimes hard to believe. This something is called *love*.

"Shiv, Veer and Aditi were my juniors in school. They played in a band in school and now they play in college. Five of us are going on our jungle concert." Before RV could finish the last word, Sonam almost screamed and engulfed the four of them in a hug. Some kids and adults who were splashing in the pool forgot their splash and looked at these five people whose energy was contagious.

"Let's order something to drink while Sonam gets her bags," Veer said as he and Aditi settled on a table for five under the palm by the pool.

"RV, how did you think all this up? How did you manage?"

"You know what Sonam, anyone who has seen your amber eyes smiling and your face displaying your rocking heart would have no choice but to do what you like."

Sonam felt beautiful, which could not be defined. She felt herself covered with some sweet honey. Her lips felt sealed with sweet honey, which would need a little effort to part. So to feel this surreal moment with a kiss was not an option. She felt the softness of the petals over which the bees swooned while they sucked nectar to manufacture honey. She felt all the colours of the flowers from which the nectar for the honey came, had come to induce colours and colours in her life.

"Go get your bags now, we should leave soon," RV told Sonam and turned to be with other band members. His full-sleeve checked shirt over a round neck T-shirt worn over tattered jeans, made him look like a rockstar already. The body language and the red cap he wore further rocked the look.

Sonam stood with her bag at the porch of the hotel with RV, Shiv, Veer and Aditi.

"How are we going guys?" Sonam looked around for a vehicle.

"Give me your bag," Shiv took her handbag and said, "The vehicle is on the road outside." Shiv's broad built made the handbag look small, which had appeared oversized in Sonam's hand. The three guys of the young band were almost of the same height, RV being slightly taller. Aditi was around five feet three inches tall, slim enough for the shorts she wore. She wore a bandana which let out her hair to touch her shoulders. Sonam's mind was home to all beautiful thoughts and no interrogative questions were allowed there, like where they were going or how they would manage. RV had completely earned her trust.

When RV and the rest of them stopped in front of the Indian Tata truck, Shiv hurled her bag into it. Sonam's eyes and mouth opened in surprise as her hands cupped her cheeks. She sucked in some air to take in this extra dose of surprise. She admired their rock band truck to believe whatever was happening was real.

RV had already jumped on the truck and gave a hand to the girls to help them climb. "We have sleeping bags, tents, bongo-drums, Spanish guitar, conga, maraca, tambourine..." Shiv, Arti and Veer pitched in to introduce their prized possessions in their music caravan.

"Who is going to drive?" Sonam asked.

"We will take turns to drive," RV said putting his hand over Shiv's shoulders, while Veer held RV's shoulders from the back.

"So that leaves us with the job of a cleaner," Aditi said keeping her elbow over Sonam's shoulders.

"RV, I want to drive first," Shiv took the truck keys from Rann Vijay.

The truck looked quite cosy on the inside, with mattresses covering most of the area. Sonam took off her slippers like everybody else. Pillows and colourful cushions were thrown over plain cotton bed sheets which covered the mattresses. The music instruments were kept there. There were two heavy wooden boxes, one for some dry snacks and the other for some delicate stuff for the band.

Sonam picked up the Spanish guitar, held it like a typical rock star and used the sticker to play the strings and sang, "Bilando… oo..ooo…" as the truck started. Aditi joined on the drums, RV took the maraca and everyone sang.

"Yeah! Yeah, three cheers to our jungle band." Shiv honked the horn three four times to add to the music. Veer took his hand out of the window and banged on the truck's body to set it into musical ripples. The rays of the sun rocked and its face flushed. The truck was out of Jaipur now and en route to Pushkar. The actual playing of the music had stopped now, but guitar and drums played in their hearts, soaking them with the appreciation of actually being on this rocking trip.

RV stood on one of the wooden boxes which made him stand taller than the hood of the truck. He looked at the road ahead and the new landscape that sprang on both the sides. Sonam sat on the floor of the truck on the mattress, with her back resting against the body of the truck, encircling the guitar in her arms; holding on to this good time, feeling it was real.

"Sonam, this song is easy to play. I will teach you," Aditi came and sat besides Sonam, bringing with her two cushions and her guitar book."

"You think so, Aditi?" Sonam asked as she adjusted one cushion behind her back.

"Of course, the way you moved your fingers on the strings spoke well of your knowledge."

"Yeah! I played a little in our music classes in school."

Music brought Rann Vijay back inside the truck. "Wait! Aditi, I am also coming," RV said as he picked up another guitar and sat next to Aditi.

While RV and Sonam were trying to figure out various notes, the breeze had already figured it out, as it blew playing fast rocking number over this moving truck. When a person goes away from a long time relation and is not close enough to a new one, it feels dull. This is how the earth feels during dusk – the sun is leaving it and the night has not hugged her. The rock band truck was passing through dusk now. The dullness of the dusk was picked up by the sticker of the guitar, turning it into beautiful notes of music, which danced over the dullness, crushing it completely.

"Sonam press this A, then H.." Aditi pulled Sonam back, as she was lost in the dullness of images she was used to seeing in the evenings before.

"It is dark, can't play now." Sonam kept the guitar aside while wearing a disappointed look.

"Aditi, come let's get the lights," RV asked Aditi.

"You have lights here!" Sonam said.

RV and Aditi started to spread the wire of white fairy lights and when they plugged it to a battery bank, the whole truck glowed and Aditi stood on the wooden box. Sonam just sat, while her eyes picked up dreams and happiness from the lights.

"Let's continue the practice," RV said, giving her the guitar back. Sonam looked into RV's eyes and said, "Didn't know my amber eyes could get so much done."

"They are capable of much more." RV gave a killing smile, complimenting Sonam's naughty smile.

The road was almost traffic free. Good shockers of the truck ensured a smooth ride. As Sonam got comfortable with the guitar, she started singing.

Mainu aho truck chahida
Tera naal sath chahida (Sonam's smile also complimented the lyrics.)
Bolne di lorh koi na – RV joined as he played the guitar.
Dabbi vergi akh khol ke
Ambara nu vi dendi ha chuka
Oye hoe – Sonam sang
Eh tah thorha jada ho gaya – Sonam replied
Oye nhi (RV pitched in)
Aje gal dabbi khulan tak di
Akh de rang di tahn kahani baki hai
Oye pher truck lamba challuga (Sonam replied)
Nal nal drum vajjange – RV sang
Maraca da ve sath rahu ga – Sonam pitched in
Highway te truck tappda – RV
Jungla ch mor nachda – Sonam
Lighta ch tare vasde
Truck nu japhi pa ke
Kush ho tim tim kar de
Chava de nal chava bajuga – RV pepped it up further
Dhamal he dhamal machuga
Oye shava, oye shava... (Aditi also joined in, who was only enjoying listening till now.)

Oye shava. Veer started singing in a peppy tune as he had jumped in when the truck stopped.

Shava, o shava, O shava..... Shiv was the last one to join as he took some time to stop the truck at a roadside dhaba and take out the key.

Everyone clapped and Sonam and RV also kept the guitar aside to clap with everyone.

"Our rock band has started with a bang." Shiv looked visibly excited.

"We have earned ourselves a dinner, guys," Aditi said.

"Dinner at eleven at a dhabha, what more can we ask for," Veer said while he took out his bandana, ran his fingers in his hair as if trying to wake them up.

"You guys sing well. Your Punjabi is quite good. RV, your mom is Punjabi, I know. And Sonam, what about you?" Veer asked.

"Yeah! I am a Punjabi," Sonam said.

"Punjabi is anyway almost like a national language. Mostly many songs in Hindi movies these days are in Punjabi," Aditi said as she sat on the charpoy of the dhaba.

"Guys you order, anything is fine with me," Shiv said as he laid down on one of the charpoys and took out his Nike head band to free his curled hair to venture over his fair forehead. Shiv's eyes were caressed by the cool night breeze as he watched the neem leaves sway on the huge neem tree which stood at the corner of the dhaba.

Aditi and Sonam constantly laughed and chirped, making up for the birds which lay cosy into their nest at night.

"What will you have, Aditi and Sonam?" RV called out as he was giving the food order to the dhaba boy.

"Anything vegetarian," they shouted back and got back to their interesting conversation.

"I will help you bhai." Veer kept his elbow over RV's shoulder and they ordered a few starters – Tandoori special and of course the famous highway dal – all vegetarian.

When Sonam looked up while talking to Aditi, she saw that RV had tied his shirt over his waist and his T-shirt flaunted the V cut of his body. Her dreams expanded with a few more colourful strokes.

"Hey boy! What's your name?" RV asked and said, "I will help you. Give me the plates, I'll take."

"I am Bhola, sir."

"Okay Bhola, give me this water jug too," Sonam said as she joined RV and turned the rim of RV's cap back as a gesture to compliment his good looks and which spoke of her affection too.

As Sonam sipped fresh lime, which was the last course of the meal, she said, "This platform under the neem tree is perfect for our band to play."

Aditi looked from above the rim of her glass to see what Sonam was talking about. "Mind-blowing! This is perfect to start our first show."

The way Shiv slipped the head band over his head spoke of his take on the idea.

"Veer, let's get the drums down from the truck." Shiv jumped on to the truck and passed the drums to Veer.

"Bhaiya, we will entertain you and your guests tonight," Veer called out to the owner of the dhaba."

"Wah ji, wah! I will keep the dhaba open till you play."

Bhola in his fifteen years of life had not felt this good. When he came to take the utensils, he held his steel tray in one hand and his right hand automatically started to play on the tray as he watched the arrangements of the rock show.

"Bhola, I will keep these plates back. You join us for the band," RV said taking the tray from him.

"I don't know how to play, sir."

"Many of us here don't know. Our band is basically to feel the joy of being in the band. We will give you something simple to play. Play the way you feel like. There is nothing right or wrong here. So, chill."

"Shiv, give him the maraca and tell him the basics." Bhola was sucked in by the enthusiasm of the band.

Sonam watched RV's conversation with Bhola and she felt she was falling for him all over again. Right now, she saw a different lovely shade of RV.

Tuning in the guitar, Aditi set the mood of the night. Shiv got busy with hanging glass shades, some round and some elongated and inserted some fairy lights into them on the neem tree.

"Those wooden boxes have these things?" Sonam said with a smile, which could only be seen in fairy lands. The stage of the jungle band directly overlooked the side wall of the dhaba.

"Veer, sing some Latin American numbers," Sonam called out to Veer who was taking off his denim jacket to give his arms more mobility in a T-shirt.

"Okay Sonam."

"RV, please help me take this charpoy near the wall," Sonam said.

"Yes, we can lean against the wall," RV said as he helped her take the charpoy.

Shiv played the drums, Aditi supported with guitar, Veer was at tambourine, all singing Bilando. The breeze was also still, listening to this music. When something is done with passion and not for anything commercial, the end product is always surreal. Bhola was trying something with the maraca. There was enough space between Sonam and RV's shoulders, but the radiation of love entered inside them, bringing their dreams to reality. They clicked their index finger and thumb together to make a click sound while swaying. As the night progressed, she snuggled closer to RV, and kept her head on his shoulders.

It was one in the night. They had enjoyed many songs by now.

The dhabha person got hot tea for everyone with biscuits. "How very considerate of you!" Aditi said after taking a glass and biscuits.

"The tea is awesome," Shiv and Veer said after taking a sip.

"This is the least I could do for the entertainment you brought to my small dhabha."

Sonam got up to take her tea and said, "Having tea like this is so satisfying; now imagine having one on a foggy night."

RV just held on to the tea glass without sipping.

"Hello! RV, where are you? Not having tea?" Sonam asked.

RV didn't say anything, but he was thinking if and when those winter nights would come.

"Hey, take this bedsheet if you want to and the cushions for your back," Shiv said hurling those towards them. He had pulled these along when he had got some more biscuits from the truck.

"Guys, by two, we will start for a resort at Pushkar. We will go sleep there," RV, announced as he adjusted the cushions for himself and Sonam.

"What fun if we stay awake at night and sleep during the day!" Sonam said.

"Yes, sleep late then swim, eat, and by four we will go out somewhere, as it will be hot before that and we don't keep anything fixed. We will do whatever we feel like."

"All this will cost a lot of money," Sonam asked.

"Yeah! we will all contribute," RV said, even though he wanted to say how can I take money from you when you are such a great companion.

"Dutch is the only way fair enough, but I can never pay you for this grand 'trucks and trucks of fun'," Sonam said.

"Sonam has given a great name to our tour – Trucks and trucks of fun," RV said. They all enjoyed trucks and trucks of laughter.

"Come guys, let's play some more music. RV will sing the song which we practiced in the truck. Please give me something to play," Sonam said. They gave her a tambourine.

They played and sang, just for the simple thrill of music and being themselves. There was no fear of being judged as the audience were the trees, shrubs, stars and moon. Why can't we always be ourselves without being judged?

6

Sonam scurried down the steps of her cottage at Pushkar on the first floor the next morning. They had reached at three in the morning and Sonam could not wait to see the resort in the day light. She walked into a huge lawn as her loose frock tried to stretch out its wrinkles of the night. A few coconut trees grew there, which looked confused looking at the man-made oasis – swimming pool.

The coconut trees were not very big, so with a little jump, Sonam was able to take out one big leaf. The leaf enjoyed its dip in the pool as Sonam sat on the rim with her feet dipped in the pool, while she swayed the leaf in the water. She swayed her legs along with the leaf. She saw a piece of paper and was thinking how she should get it without getting up when she saw Rann Vijay coming in denim shorts and a T-shirt.

"RV, get that paper here!" she told RV.

"Why do you need this paper?" RV asked dipping his legs in the pool and sat next to Sonam.

"Make a boat," she told him.

"With this paper?" RV asked.

"Of course," Sonam took a tiny little boat which RV made and placed it on the coconut leaf. Then she continued to swaying the leaf with the boat on it.

"You don't plan to leave the boat in the water?" RV asked.

"I will, after making the boat enjoy this ride on the leaf," Sonam said.

RV also started swaying his legs in water like Sonam did. "I am sure this is to make the ride more exciting," RV said, raising his eyebrows towards their feet movement and smiling.

"Yes," said Sonam. Their feet touched each other's and the two pair of feet moved together. They increased the speed. RV slid his hand on her waist, encircling from behind. She felt the current which gave better sound than an electric guitar. Sonam also slid her hand around RV's waist thinking that two guitars playing together would always be better. Made sense because it was a music tour anyway.

"You know what RV." Sonam forgot what she was going to say and both just looked at each other. RV's right hand lifted to touch her cheek. Their lips prepared, waiting to meet each other.

"RV, the boat," Sonam ditched her lips.

"Oh! The boat," RV obeyed his ears and ignored his lips.

When they looked at the boat, it had turned upside down in the water. Both jumped inside together with arms still around their waist. RV inverted the boat straight. Sonam kept her hand on his shoulders and tightened her hands as he tightened his hands on the waist. It was forenoon on a hot day at the resort, so no one was out of their air-conditioned rooms.

Sonam loosened her grip and said, "You know why I hugged you?"

"Yes, because I saved your boat."

She held his hand and looked at the cute white sailing boat and said, "Our boat."

"We should go change before any of the resort people point out that we are in the pool and not in our swimming costumes," RV said as he came out of the pool. "Come, Sonam," RV said. She just stood in the pool looking at him."Come out, what happened?"

"RV, my clothes are all wet, how will I go back to my room?"

"There is no one around," RV said.

"Then lift me and take me," Sonam said.

"Lift you? No, you are too heavy!"

"I am heavy, ok... then I will lift you." Sonam came out with one jump and tried to lift him, holding from his waist.

In one scoop, RV lifted Sonam in both his arms. "You are naughtier than I thought," RV said looking at this beautiful wet girl in his arms.

"Yes, the coconut tree leaves also think so," Sonam said as she circled her arms around his neck like a garland.

He was climbing the stairs of her cottage. "Thank you so much, you can leave me outside my door now." RV looked into her innocent amber eyes and put her down.

"I will go and get the gang ready too, and let's play some games in the games room." RV was already down when he said the last word.

RV had armed his cue to hit the red ball when he saw Sonam entering the games room dressed in ruffled dress. The off shoulder dress bared her shoulders like the petals bare a pure flawless bud. RV forgot about hitting the ball and stood with cue in his hand.

“RV, let’s play the good old carrom. My mom used to play in her childhood.”

“Then she played with you?” RV asked.

“No, she stayed very busy.”

“Your mom works?” RV asked adjusting the carom table.

“No, but still is very busy,” Sonam said.

“Hi, you all came at the right time. Let’s play carrom,” Sonam said when she saw Shiv and Aditi coming.

“Where is Veer?” RV asked

“Call him RV, check if he got up,” Aditi said.

RV was just dialling the number when he saw Veer coming. “Four of you play. I will make sure no one cheats,” said RV.

“Yeah! The Rani is mine,” said Sonam as she raised her arms to celebrate.

‘What? Is Sonam talking on my behalf?’

“Enough of this game! I am hungry now,” Aditi said.

“Yes, all of us are,” RV said.

“Sonam, are you visiting Pushkar for the first time?” Veer asked.

“Yup.”

“Then you must go and visit the city,” Shiv said.

“You can get mind blowing silver jewellery here,” Aditi added.

“You girls always think of shopping!” Shiv said.

“Ha ha ha! As if you boys don’t buy expensive shoes and clothes…”Aditi replied.

“Relax guys, the discussion was about planning something for Sonam. Our truck would be too small for a city visit and getting a mobike for hire would be the easiest option.” Veer suggested.

"RV, you and Sonam go. You know,we are too lazy. We all will sleep and laze around in the pool," Aditi said.

The planning was complete by the time the dessert arrived. They hired a Bullet from a motorbike hiring service.

"Five is the perfect time to leave," RV said.

"How will I sit on a bike with this frock?" Sonam asked as RV and Sonam were standing near the Bullet on an almost empty road outside the resort.

"Sit with both the legs on one side, the bazaar is not too far and I will drive slow."

"No RV, you must drive very fast. Why should we miss the thrill because of some stupid fears? Life has to be lived to the fullest." Sonam stood while resting her foot on either side of the foot rest. She held on to RV's shoulders and enjoyed the cool breeze against her face.

"Sonam, the next thing would be you standing on the seat."

"This is exactly what I was thinking."

RV abruptly stopped the bike and said, "Get down, Sonam!"

"Okay okay! I won't stand on the bike."

RV put on his killing smile and said, "We need to walk now. The bazzar is just here."

"Oh!" Sonam said as she got down. "I made the ride interesting. Now, RV, it's your turn to make the bazaar interesting."

"I will pick up some silver jewellery and start running and you start shouting Chor! Chor!" RV said.

"No use! These firang girls will hound you; they would not have seen such a stunning guy," Sonam said.

"What better way to make this evening thrilling? I will get to flirt with so many firangi girls!" RV said.

"No, even better would be if I run with the silver neck piece of my choice. After all, there are so many guys here," Sonam said in a spicy tone.

"Ok truce!" RV said and pulled her closer. He kept his arm over her shoulders and walked on to explore the narrow lanes of Pushkar.

"Do you really think I am so good looking?" RV asked

"Of course! You forgot my kiss on your cheek?"

RV bent down and gave a loud kiss on her cheek. "Sorry, I am late in putting a seal to your good looks," and continued walking.

Sonam could not understand how this appreciative kiss could be so passionate. Her cheeks became hot. She could not remember which cheek he kissed as both the cheeks were equally hot. Before she could take herself out of the confusion of the cheek, her whole body radiated heat.

"Let's see this shop," RV said, leading her to a small shop. "You Portugal?" the overfriendly shopkeeper greeted them and spoke in Portuguese.

"No, we are from England," Sonam said.

The language of the shopkeeper changed to British accent as he showed different things.

Sonam tried one Topaz-studded silver bracelet.

"We are buying this bracelet." RV paid and she put it on. "This is a present," RV said and the bracelet which hung in her wrist touched RV's wrist in affirmation for accepting the gift as they walked hand in hand to explore. It was all dark now.

"Sonam, you will love this Camel cart ride." RV recalled when he saw some toy-stuffed camels hanging from a shop at the bazar. They almost ran to their bike and they were off to the ride place. Most of the camel carts had gone by now.

Both RV and Sonam sat on either side of the cart driver, facing ahead with the camel and held on the poles as the caravan rocked on the sand. The sand became visible wherever the moonlight walked.

"Bhai ! Please teach me how to drive this caravan."

"Yes bhaiya, give her the reins of the camel. She is going to take this job of taking tourists for a ride."

"Yes bhaiya, can you help me get one caravan on hire? I don't have any job," Sonam was at her naughty best.

The boy looked totally confused but he took Sonam as his student. The boy gave Sonam the reins and started to explain while the caravan was driven by Sonam. RV enjoyed the ride as he watched Sonam and her enthusiasm for life.

Now Sonam exchanged places with the caravan driver. "Chuck, chuck.." She was making the sounds too that the camel could understand and she bent forward to pat the animal.

"Thank you so much bhaiya for teaching me. Very soon I will come to you for helping me hire one."

"Bye," RV said and pulled Sonam down. "Don't tell me you want to take this up as a job."

"No harm. I want a job that gives me thrill. I cannot do something which gets monotonous. Someday I may do this for a change to earn money," Sonam said.

"I agree to this. I also don't want to spend my life getting orders for our diamond business. My mom and dad wanted me to come with them to Belgium to help them host the exhibition. But I can't always be surrounded with diamonds," RV told Sonam.

"You are doing the right thing," Sonam agreed.

"I want to make a living in India. Most of our business is abroad, so my parents stay abroad for about 300 days in a year," RV told Sonam.

"India is the best. See the number of foreign tourists who come here!" Sonam said.

"The shopkeepers know so many languages here just by talking to them. Look at the level of intelligence we have in India," RV said as they reached near their bike.

"RV, let's call our gang for dinner."

RV dialled a number and said, "Shiv, all of you come at the restaurant in front of Pushkar Lake."

Five of them sat at the table placed outside the restaurant.

'Someone has well thought to put these bulbs all around the lake. They look like diyas.' Sonam admired the bulbs, and the soft light being reflected in the water as she sipped her fresh lime.

"Sonam, you should visit during the Pushkar fair; it is an awesome experience!" Veer suggested, popping up another veg manchurian.

"I will definitely come for the Pushkar fair if you all promise to take me in our truck."

"Of course," they all said in unison.

"Cheers to our truck band," they clinked their glasses together, gulping down their doubts if they would be together in winters. But the doubt rose and bubbled like the soda of fresh lime.

7

"Where are we going to perform today?" Sonam asked as they did their fun rehearsal of a Punjabi song with music. Every shrub bared itself to the minutest detail in the glowing evening sun.

"Deogarh Fort," RV said.

"You mean we have to actually perform?" Sonam could not hide her disappointment.

"No, no, it is a small fort, owner is a friend. He told me only a few foreigners are there at this time of the year. Don't worry Sonam. I know what you want."

'What I want! I want this trip to become a trip of a whole life. Oh! I am becoming too greedy.' Sonam thought as she kept her folded arms on the side rim of the truck and rested her cheek on them. The beauty of the landscape erased all the questions of her mind. 'Let me just enjoy this time which is all mine.' She held the rim with both her hands and swung back looking up at the blue mixed with red, the massiveness of the sky given approachability by the low lying clouds. RV was busy discussing the exciting play of the band at the Deogarh fort with others when his eye caught Sonam's date with the sky. He felt like stealing the sky's date and wondered how could the clouds not come down and resist Sonam's lips.

Aditi and Sonam stood next to each other on the wooden truck looking over the crown of the truck getting curious to see the fort as the truck rode in the sleepy town. The twists and turns of the narrow lanes kept feeding and teasing their curiosity. Shiv and RV sat on the mattress of the truck, relaxed, leaning against the cushions as they had been to Deogarh Fort before. The truck climbed the gradient when Sonam's eyes caught something shiny in bright light.

"What was this shiny thing?" And before Sonam could guess anything, they were in front of a huge gate of Deogarh Fort. They all jumped off the truck and entered the big gate.The huge door opened to a fountain at the foot of the fort.

"Hi Rohan," RV greeted a young man. "Rohan, this is Aditi, Shiv, Veer and Sonam."

"Hi everybody, give me and this fort a rocking time, play wherever you feel like," Rohan said in a friendly manner. He saw Sonam looking up, her eyes climbing the stair case.

"Yes Sonam, play up there, that is the place I also had in mind," Rohan said.

"Perfect!" RV said.

Sonam quickly climbed up. Apart from the adventure of climbing to the top, Sonam wanted to see what was that shiny thing embedded on top of the fort. When Sonam reached the top, she was greeted by narrow passage done in stone which opened in semi circles. The place spoke of power the army must have felt when it walked over it. Today the truck band people felt this power and the power they already had in themselves to lead a life at their own terms.

Tan, ta tin.. the strings broke out into a powerful melody when Sonam and RV played the guitar together and the drums played by Aditi and Shiv declared, 'Hey life! We have arrived.' Veer set the metal jingles of the tambourine into a riot of music. Sonam could see thikri work mural on the fort building and could feel the music do a little tango with the glitter. The music by this truck band played continuously for some time. The five musicians were one with their music when Rohan, the waiters and some guests sitting on the stairs started clapping. The applause was for their music, passion, no botheration of being judged, togetherness and their friendship.

"You guys are great," Rohan said. "Have something before you start your next music."

RV and Sonam stood at opposite sides leaning on the wall, which was just enough to support and did not hide the view.

"Menu eho truck chahida… Tera nal sath chahida," Sonam started and the flow of music took her to the centre while she sang. RV came near her while he sang and shifted the mike in his left hand to put his arm around her neck. They sang together and then moved to be with Shiv, Aditi, Veer and Rohan swaying and pointing the mike towards them to sing. *"Dhamal hi dhamal machugaa,"* all sing together to make a dhamal, sharing mikes to create a high-pitched full-throated finale. Then they all clapped for themselves with their face shining red as the sweat fell.

"I am not letting you all go so soon," Rohan said as he himself was bored of the routine at the hotel.

"Rohan, boss, we have no plans, we are acting on an impulse," and took his eyes off Rohan for a few seconds to look at Sonam and smiled through them.

"This is the sole purpose of this trip," Shiv and Veer pitched in.

"If you offer us something interesting, we will stay. What say, friends?" RV said.

"Right," Aditi agreed.

"Cool then," Rohan said. "We will do a fun photo shoot with you all. I want to change the mood of our fort. I will display these photos at the fort. Give me a few nights of music, not like a performance, just music for the sake of music."

"Rohan, we are more than convinced now. Show us our rooms. We will choose the best ones," Aditi and Veer said.

"The fort is all yours," Rohan said. "Early morning light, say six is great for photography, so whoever makes it by then is great, for the rest any time of the day also is okay. I will tell our in-house photographer."

"Dude, you are making us feel the celebrity part of a band," Veer said.

"You guys are coming up with such an original idea, so you are real celebrities," Rohan said as he led them inside the fort. "These are the rooms… take whichever you like."

The thikri work on top of the fort indulged in vigorous game of red marbles with the early rays of the sun. When RV looked down, he saw Sonam in some discussion with the camera guy. Approacing closer, he saw Sonam flap her hand in the water of a big urn in which red lotus popped their head. After creating big ripples in the water, Sonam took her pose of a rockstar holding the guitar. A silver loop of red beads clung to her belly button, which stood between her angel-sleeved white top and faded shorts.

"No, the ripples become weak in the photo," said Sonam when she looked into the camera.

"You just pose Sonam. I will create ripples." Sonam used her fingers to bring her front step of hair to fall in style, brought a little attitude to her neck and posed playing the guitar which hung across her body. RV flapped his hand in the water and hid behind the big urn and the photo was perfect. RV had just transferred some of the ripples which were created looking at Sonam, into the water.

"You got the ripples just perfect," the photographer said. "Hi, I am Ravi."

"Hi brother! I am Rann Vijay. Thanks for making us feel like celebrities," RV said extending his hand for him.

"RV! I will suggest a pose for you." Sonam bubbled with ideas. "Stand on this old stone wall." RV jumped up and spread his hands, raising his chin just enough to meet the rising sun. His guitar clung like his black vest and flowed with his black ripped jeans. This was not a pose, but an aura of the wall well-shown. The cameraman captured the beauty and spirit bringing out the golden yellow hue of RV's hair, which ruffled as per their own wish.

"Wait RV! I will also come on this wall." And they leaned back to back for a few clicks.

Shiv and Veer had come with their set of drums. "Where is Aditi?" Sonam asked

"I am here," Aditi sat on the top stair with two maracas.

After everyone's individual photoshoot, the whole gang sat on the stairs spreading after Aditi and they all were captured in one frame.

"Let's go for breakfast," Shiv suggested.

"Yes! Rohan will finish his work and join us there," RV said after checking with him on phone and they walked towards the fort restaurant. The restaurant interiors fuelled their imagination and certainly did not fence anything. Everyone was taking a little of everything in their plate, more like a childlike joy of grabbing everything and not to satisfy their hunger.

"Hi guys ! I came to know of your great photoshoot!" Rohan also came and clicked his hand with theirs at whatever angle and position they were offered. We all will have some fun with music in the evening. I have named it – 'IMPULSE'."

"Superb!" RV said.

"I just want my fort to come alive with real music, laughter and claps which come from the heart and not any forced applause," Rohan said, sipping fresh orange juice occasionally.

"Done," the six of them hit their fists together to create an energy pool.

"Enjoy your day guys. See you in the evening," Rohan said and left.

"Sonam, your belly button ring is so damn cute," Aditi said.

"I have another similar one. I'll give it to you, Aditi."

"Some kind of stones stuck to the belly also look rocking," Aditi shared her fashion sense. "Actually guys, we need to buy some rockstar accessories," Aditi said.

"Yeah! Aditi is right. It would be so much fun. First think how to dress up as rockstars, then of course we go buying," Veer added.

"Love you guys for coming up with such great ideas. I will buy a leather wrist band, preferably with metal studs," Shiv said.

"I am going to get a tattoo done, who all want to come?" RV said after seeing the local address for a tattoo artist on his phone.

"I am coming." Everyone said together in a happy chorus. Shiv and Sonam walked behind RV, Veer and Aditi on the narrow lanes of Deogarh. "Any place can be best discovered by foot," Sonam told Shiv as they turned with the curve of the road.

"Yes, but I always prefer walking when it is very cold, not in this heat," Shiv said as he wiped his forehead with the back of his hand, leaving a few curls of his hair still stuck to his forehead.

"Shiv, I have led a very boring life till now, so I find walking in this heat as a rebellion of my boring life and it propels me never to go back to it. I will never allow my life to get boring." Sonam's resentment tried to come out even without her trying.

"I salute the sun for making people attribute such big words, rebellion and all," Shiv said as he actually gave a nice smart salute to the sun.

"Shiv, stop pulling my leg!" Sonam ran to catch and reward him with a few boxes. He started running when he realized Sonam was coming after him. RV and the others watched them run till the end of the lane and could not see them when they turned.

RV's heart melted seeing Sonam's innocent and friendly nature. As RV walked, he wondered what would have been left of his heart at the rate it had melted from the time he met Sonam. When RV and the others also turned, they saw Sonam holding her heels in her hand, which she had removed to run fast, laughing and sharing some joke with Shiv. RV looked at

Sonam who looked all wet, and one drop of sweat had turned into a pearl in the oyster of her belly button. The silver ring of her belly button had got a pearl embedded in it. RV's eyes had slipped on to the wet sweat and found support on the pearl of her belly button. He pulled himself close to the pearl and closed the lid of the oyster, but all in his mind. This naughty thought had spread over a question which had arisen in RV's mind, 'Why was Sonam's life boring – for a bubbly girl like her?' He recalled hearing the conversation between her and Shiv.

"RV, Aditi, where are you?" Veer called out. "I have found the tattoo artist, he is just in the next lane." The conversation till the tattoo artist revolved around what tattoo everyone would get made. The ideas ranged from eagle, guitar, drums, pistols, fairy, etc.

"You all are forgetting, we are all part of a truck band, so a truck or anything related to a truck should be made," Veer said.

"I want to give you an award for this grand piece of tattoo," Aditi said as she took out her nail filer from her bag and gestured to present it to Veer.

"I will not give this back now," Veer said.

"No problem," said Aditi. "I have another one." While they joked, Shiv got started with the tattoo.

"Wait wait, we all will design for us, something with a same base but some variation for all," Aditi said. "This is the image of a Tata truck – see the front, back, side, crown and select whatever you like."

"I have selected this," Veer said.

"Show us on a paper what we explain, and please be extra careful," the girls said.

"Okay, I will draw it for you," the artist said and left his needle aside before he started making anything on Veer. Surprisingly, Veer, RV and Shiv also got interested in getting their tattoo done on a paper with their inputs. The tattoo artist changed the image they had in mind to perfection on paper. His strokes gave music to the body of the truck spreading the spirit of musical caravan to the tattoo.

Shiv was the first to get the tattoo and next was Veer, while everyone admired his tattoo. "Look at these dumbbells," said Sonam. It was a two inch Tata truck tattoo which looked out from below his shoulders with cute little dumbbells hanging from the top of the wind screen, where usually the nazar black threads hang on a real Tata truck.

"These dumbbells look apt for your well-toned biceps," Aditi said.

"Veer, you get some weights made as you spend most of your time in the gym," Aditi twisted to tell Veer.

"That is obvious." Veer added, "Aditi, see in the drawing, my truck has weights as its wheel."

"Okay!"

After getting thir tattoos made, the gang checked out the tribal jewellery at some shop on another street. While the others checked jewellery, RV and Sonam checked each other's tattoo which sat on the back of their shoulder. Both had the same shape of the truck, with two cocks facing each other on the crown of the truck. The size of RV's tattoo was two inches and Sonam's was one inch. There was one more difference – RV's tattoo had cocks' on the truck's windscreen in the shape of SS (Sonam Singh) while Sonam's tattoo had cocks spread themselves into

RV (Rann Vijay). The artist had used all his artistic skills to make SS and RV in the form of cocks that a very careful eye was needed to run over his artistry to decipher it. Both RV and Sonam could see their names in each other's tattoo the moment they saw them, although they were clever enough to tell the artist to make it so without anyone noticing it.

RV and Sonam's love had been expressed in their tattoos. But tattoos don't speak, no matter how beautifully they are made. RV and Sonam needed to put it in words. Words are important, they have the capacity to seal, to commit, and to be encashed if written on the cheque of feelings. When will Sonam and RV say it?

8

With their bags full of lot of gypsy jewellery and some other tinklets, and their stomachs full with local cuisine from a restaurant, they reached Deogarh Fort.

"Wait Veer! hold this bag," and Aditi lifted her foot to keep on the rock, to take a picture of her tattoo – cute little thing above the ankle. There was a little outline of a guitar on the wind screen of the truck. "Thanks Veer."

"They are all at the fort roof top." Veer replied to Aditi as she looked around with inquisitive eyes.

"Boss, can you get cold coffee at the roof top?" Aditi asked one of the waiters as she and Veer were climbing up.

"Ok ma'am!"

"Thanks," Aditi said.

RV was being helped by Sonam and Shiv to insert thin silver chains in his belt. "Shiv, leave two loops hanging one side and let at least four rows of chains fall from the right side of the waist." Sonam was fully involved to give RV a professional rockstar look.

"RV, you rock!" Veer commented when he and Aditi reached at the rooftop.

Shiv found a shiny black wrist band and wore it. He folded the edge of his half sleeve T-shirt and the look was complete. Guys were ready and the girls took a little longer and the truck gang actually felt like a rock band. They were at the last sip of coffee when Rohan came all excited about the fun evening at his fort.

When they entered the lawn of the fort, they almost jumped high trying to match their posters which adorned the lawn at various places. "Impulse" glittered at the backdrop of the stage in blue neon light. When they came out of the frenzy of the big posters, they realized some people, a mix of Indians and foreigners clapped for them in this place washed with bluish light with red and white spot lights thrown here and there. Sonam stood where she was while the others except RV went ahead.

RV took Sonam's hand and said, "My rockstar! Something is missing." Sonam looked into his eyes. RV put his hand in his pocket and took out a big cocktail ring in greyish metal with a big aquamarine stone embedded in it and made her wear it in her index finger. The next ring which he made her wear was five silver bands attached together. He made her wear different statement rings in almost all her fingers.

"Yes! I look like a rockstar now," she said keeping her hands on her waist, touching the gypsy necklace with chains, hanging from her waist, touching her blue skirt. And of course, the silver ring of the belly button were intact. Just then, the music started on a bang, with no warm up. It was just turned on.

RV swept his eyes over her and ran to the stage to take the mike. He had his head tilted and eyes down when the white spotlight fell on him. He started singing a rocking Latin American song. He slowly lifted his eyes, his head going with the naughtiness of the song. It was the kind of look which would penetrate anyone's heart and would lift it with the rim of his eyelashes.

Sonam jumped up. The moment her feet touched the ground, her hand went up, taken by the rocking song and music, making it move, pounding it on various notes of music which had electrified the whole place. This tantalizing music spread notes on the floor also, which screamed to be pounded to feel their energy.

RV took out the mike in a quick pluck and it was a moment when the singer talks only to the mike. The mike also got into the mood as RV swiped it to and fro, keeping it close to his lips all the while.

The beats of the Bongo drum would bring the dead to life or the living dead, punching and smacking with the beats. When Shiv's hands thumped on the Bongo, his curly hair got knocked with the same energy.

Aditi's fingers on the guitar pressed the strings and the strings got greedier for her press. The crowd of this 'impulse' gathering turned hysterical when RV reached the edge of the stage and bent on his knees turning sideways, sweeping his hands and eyes from the drummer Veer to the crowd.

The crowd hooted back, and just then, Veer's drums became even more vigrous and RV came into the crowd.

The energy of the drumsticks hitting the cymbals and the fat pedals that hit hi-hat cymbal were getting higher and higher, making Veer's triceps also throb. His thick silver chain danced over his T-shirt.

Rohan, who was in the crowd till now, started playing the keyboard kept there for anyone to play. Veer and Shiv showed him a thumbs up. Rohan enjoyed his passion, which he could not for a long time. RV's song had ended and before anyone could clap or think of the next song, Rohan started to play a tune joined by other music instruments. It was a famous duet Latin American number. RV and the crowd welcomed the song raising their hands to claps over the head. The tune stirred the heart and travelled all the way to the throat, spreading to the lungs. As if this music itself was not enough to turn everyone mad, RV started to sing. Sonam left the maraca and grabbed another mike to answer RV in the song. She walked closer towards RV in a graceful but swag walk of a rockstar. They were face to face now, their mikes almost touching each other's, answering each other in the song. RV kept his hand lightly on her stomach and Sonam took a few backward steps before lifting her arms to sway to the tune. She kept her arm over his shoulder and sang looking at the crowd. They sang together and their voice enjoyed travelling together to the crowd everywhere.

The bluish purple washed arena was punctured with red and white lights here and there. Sonam kept her hand over RV's heart while he answered with a little twitch in his brows. She started to walk towards the other end of the stage, doing full justice to her high heels and the music to which she sang. The smile which Sonam had left on RV's face was picked up by his voice as he started walking towards her and she had also turned back.

RV engulfed her neck in his elbow and the two of them together raised the pitch of the song, while the rest in the band were producing enough music to raise the song. RV sang slowly while his voice walked over the ripples created by their high pitch notes. She replied in a teasing tone which blew like a storm over these ripples. They ended the song singing over each other's shoulder.

They hugged each other tightly celebrating so many things. No one was in the mood to let go of this musical night. Aditi came with the mike and sang while playing the guitar. Dressed in a red shiny short dress, she lived her dream to feel like a rockstar. Sonam played guitar, RV played drums, while Veer, Shiv and Aditi sang another song of love and naughtiness in style, bringing all the elements of a rockstar which they ever fancied. The last song was sung by everyone together, with music of resounding sound of claps of the crowd. They danced, they hugged and swayed holding hands, yet, nothing was enough to show their euphoric state of mind and their friendship.

No one was perfect to play or sing in the truck gang, but their spirit to live their dreams was more than perfect. There is just one life. The thrill of the super successful show had already hit them like tequila shots. But there was more. People of all age groups came to take their autographs. The person who listens to his heart and allows it to be happy is a celebrity. Isn't he? Life takes autographs from him. The lights were off now, only to be filled by the moonlight. RV was overlooking the music instruments to be kept back safely in a room, while the others had gone to their rooms. But Sonam was not the one to let herself be confined to her room. So, here she was, enjoying the rose bush fragrance and colour, which could not be confined like her.

Sonam noticed that RV was free now and went to him holding a pen and paper. "I had so much fun RV," she held him from the shoulders and started jumping. She stopped when she realized her lips were too close to his. Both kissed at the same time. Too many sparks flew and yet they were clueless of what was happening.

"RV, you have also become impulsive like me," Sonam said while cheating herself into believing that the kiss was only on 'Impulse'.

"Yes Sonam, I am learning to be impulsive from you," RV replied, while his mind continued to say, 'I don't think I have justified my impulse which had urged me to explore longer.'

Their bodies simmered in a heat which hoped to cool down in silver moon light, but here, the silver too was steaming hot. The heat from their body clashed with the heat from moonlight, like swords of brave warriors. The clash only generated more heat.

'My body is more impulsive than me. Now my impulses will control that of my body,' Sonam spoke to herself, not because she wanted to act mature, but because she wanted to enjoy this simmering. Relations stay raw if not allowed to simmer.

"RV, give me your autograph please," she offered him a pen and paper. RV took the paper from her and smiled to himself as he thought, 'What if the paper catches fire?'

"So you certify me as a rockstar?" RV asked.

"I certify you for many things."

Before he could ask why she asked, "How did you know this Latin American song was the one I always imagined myself singing whenever I watched it?"

"This is my favourite song too, and I have sung it at many college fests before," RV replied.

"So you have sung this with someone before?" Sonam asked.

"No, I imagined someone like you singing with me," RV said and started writing.

To the Rockstar of my life

Love,

Rann Vijay Rathore

As Sonam took the paper she wondered whether this love was 'the' love or the customary love people write for autographs. 'Why is it so important for me to know if I was first to sing the favourite song with him?'

Before she would drown herself with these questions, RV said, "Where is my autograph?" He took out a paper from his pocket.

"Some other time," Sonam said with a smile playing on her lips.

"Sonam, you always have your way," RV said putting the paper back in his pocket.

"It's a promise." Sonam kept her hands on his cheeks and slid them down. RV's late into the night growth of stubble gave his face and Sonam's hand a new sensation, begging them for something more.

9

The night parted to give way to the sun. RV and Sonam reached the roof top almost at the same time. They were not there early morning to see the sunrise, but were here in the hope to see each other. "Sonam, Sonam," RV said, but Sonam was smiling which grooved with her shoulders. She gave a little circle to her waist and hit RV like a ball as he stood next to her.

"RV, I am in a spell of this musical time," Sonam said as they both stood near the wall looking at the sky.

"Sonam, I don't know for how many days you have come for this holiday. But I made this program thinking that even if you came for only a few days, you would extend," RV tried to swallow his doubts as his Adams' apple moved.

"I am here for a month," she said and RV hit his side bum with her's, lifting his hands too in celebration of the good news.

"So, we have a month!" both said together, turned to look at each other and hit their hands in a high-five before hitting them in a fist.

"No planning for the days ahead," Sonam said.

"No plans," RV added.

"It is not very hot today, I want to go for a bike ride, RV."

"We will take Rohan's bike. Let's go, our gang also suggested last night that I should take you out to see the area around." When Sonam went down the stairs, the bounce of her feet made her top carelessly droop from the shoulder and her tatoo winked at RV who came down the stairs behind her. The Bullet ran on some countryside road. The Aravallis wore a summer carnival look where the trees chilled out in scanty clothes. Some trees wore bright hot flowers and the branches showed off their accessories of scarves of flowers tied to them.

"Wait RV, I want to get that flower," Sonam said.

"Where is the flower?" RV asked stopping the bike.

"See, up there," she pointed to a flame of forest tree on top of the hillock which blushed to a crimson red because of the attention it got from the rest of the forest.

"Are you sure you want to climb all the way up?" RV did not see any thrill in it.

"Come, it will be fun," Sonam pulled RV's hand and he extended the other hand to take the key. 'I was right when I thought there would be no thrill. It is bending towards electrifying.' RV indulged in a little conversation with himself as they both walked over the space provided by the shrubs and a few trees.

"Everyday should be different and fun. I hate monotony." Sonam left his hand only to hold his shoulders from the back to enjoy the little gradient of the hillock.

"Don't worry, your impulse will not let that happen," RV said.

"No, I have not been able to act on impulses."

"Really?" RV asked.

"Until a few days back," Sonam completed her sentence. "Otherwise my life has been very monotonous," she explained.

RV stopped, turned around and kept his hand on her shoulders. "Tell me what it is Sonam. The other day also you said your life was too boring."

"And I also said I won't let that happen again. I don't want to talk about it and transport that boring feeling now. Forget it," Sonam said.

"Fine, take an oath here, on this hillock that you will never ever let your life get boring," RV said changing the topic.

She extended her hand in the oath taking gesture and said, "I will always have fun." RV and Sonam laughed together and the oath was already working.

"You are one and only in this world," RV said pulling her in an embrace while Sonam's hands circled his neck. The sun rose high in the sky. RV kissed on her head and eased the hug. The kiss broke the seed coat and love sprouted.

"RV, let's run till that tree," Sonam said and started running. Both reached the tree together. "RV wait, you don't pluck the flowers; I want to pluck," and she started jumping up, trying to reach them.

RV leaned against the big rock with his eyes loaded on the truck tatoo on her shoulder. His lips yearned to feel the softness and the thrill trapped in this tatoo, but he gulped down the thought and looked up when he realized that Sonam's hand still did not reach the flowers.

RV lifted her from the waist and she plucked a bunch of four. RV took two flowers and tucked them behind her ear. The other two he tucked in her front jeans pocket. The flame red against the faded blue gave a new meaning to her jeans.

"RV, you have perfectly understood my thinking of newness in life," Sonam said as they walked back to their bike. "Let's stop at some village shop if there is a village nearby. I want to buy hair pins to keep the flowers in place."

"Yes there is one nearby," RV replied. Sonam delicately held the stem of the flowers so that they do not fly away while they drove.

RV stopped when he saw a few houses."You saved my flowers," RV said when he looked at her shapely fingers holding the stem.

"I will never let go of anything that you give me," Sonam replied.

RV took two pins from the small makeshift shop and fixed the flowers. RV's stubble which he had decided to keep after Sonam's casual touch last night had trapped her attention while he fastened her pins. She rubbed her cheek on his in quick grate.

"What was this?" RV teased.

"Impulsive, thank you," Sonam replied. The prick of the stubble injected a drug in both of them, making them feel light, drowsy with something.

"RV, why can't life be full of pleasant surprises?" Sonam said.

"My life is enfolding sound, colour and light every moment from the time I have met you," RV said.

"At light and sound show!" Sonam completed with a naughty look.

RV felt a very strong need to hide that embarrassment of his drunken state on that day behind tree leaves. There were not enough leaves also on the trees, so what could he do? RV stood near the shop, thinking how he would never let that happen to him again.

"Here RV, take this pinwheel." She gave RV a pinwheel, also holding one herself which she bought from a village boy selling on the cycle. She raised the pinwheel up, offering it to the wind to put it in a groove, totally trusting the wind.

Let's see whose pinwheel grooves better," she challenged him with a little raise of her eyebrow. RV's eyebrow replied with a raise as well and both ran together. They ran watching the wheels of the pinwheel thudding on the wind, rocking all the way.

"They stopped, panting while inhaling the meaning to their own question in quick breaths – life can be full of pleasant surprises if we give momentum to small moments for fun unlimited. The sun was nicely settled with its more than half day's work and blowed out a heat of satisfaction. RV and Sonam zoomed on their bike, not looking for pleasant surprises, but creating them. Their bike entered an avenue of huge Banyan trees. The sun rays got busy tickling the leaves of the Banyan and only their laughter was spilled by the rays on the road.

"RV, please slow down the bike," Sonam said.

"Am I driving too fast?"

"No, only for a minute. I want to rest my back on yours and look back," Sonam replied. RV stopped with a sudden brake.

"Sonam I want you safe as I will not get a replacement for our band. I don't want to spoil the band," RV said wiping any grin from his face.

"Now I will definitely sit like this," as she turned and sat looking back and beaming a winning smile.

The banyans were also amused looking at her cute pose and RV's expressions. RV took out his light denim shirt, hurled it across her stomach and tied the sleeves tightly on his stomach, to support her back against his. Her tatoo now beamed as her broad neck slid down, almost kissing RV's tattoo which his black vest presented. With her feet still on the foot hold, she threw her hands on RV's shoulders. She blew a flying kiss at the berries which blushed to red. Sonam started singing,

"O berries! O berries!
Look away look away,
otherwise
You will fall a fall a fall.
Over RV!
Save yourself save your crush!
You will get crushed cru shed!" (Sonam sang while swaying, looking at the berries hanging from the canopy formed by the banyan trees.

RV joined in.
"No no no no no
RV will enjoy
The crush Cr. Cr. ush ush
I can see your blush blu blu ush ush
Make me go gu gu gush gush
Over you you you you you!"
(RV's shoulders synchronized their sway with Sonam's.)

Sonam left RV's shoulders alternating happy claps and clicking of fingers while she sang

"Oh, berry! Oh berry!
Don't tr.. ust ust
Save your crush ush ush…"

Sonam plucked her finger at the tied shirt just once as she sang.

"He has a link ink ink
You will be in a fi.. ix
Don't fa.. all.. all
Save your crush ush!" (While her clapping and clicking of fingers produced a tapping music, her feet tapped at the foot rest, also catching the foot tapping tune.
"Don't save your crush." (RV sang.)
"I say save ave.. ave" (Sonam sang.)
"Don't berry don't" (RV sang)
"Save your crush!" (Sonam sang)

This time, RV pressed his head back on her head as an answer. Sonam now just listened to the humming of her body till they reached a restaurant at the top of the hillock. Jacaranda trees around this restaurant were huge and got greedy with its flowers. These trees hurled a few violet frisbees of their flowers across to the nearby hillocks and the slope down on their sister trees. Hollowed tree trunk planters seemed to collect these flowers blown by the wind.

"These are actually petunia and not blown flowers of Jacaranda trees," Sonam called out to RV who was wearing his shirt.

"Oh really?" he said as he folded his sleeves. He also came to check the overflowing planters of purplish petunias. Their phones waited in their pockets while they clicked with their hearts and eyes.

The Greek white paint of the porch had been stirred with pounded glass, which gave the paint the sprinkle of silver. The restaurant looked like a cloud with the silver lining wandering over the hillock. The walls inside the restaurant were all glass. They sat on a long table with bar stools. The outside view also seemed to be AC blown as they looked out.

"Get me a cold coffee with ice cream," Sonam ordered.

"Make it two," RV added.

"Sure sir. We have a canvas here, sir. You can paint something," he pointed to a few empty canvas resting on easels.

"I will paint." Sonam hopped down her stool. Mirror balls also hung till the level of the canvas. The sun was in a mood to paint and sprayed orangish, yellowish paint on earth and used a few strokes of orangish red on the sky. She looked out at the scenery and painted taking most of it from there and adding her own special effects. RV stood by the canvas holding the cold coffee, occasionally making her sip as she painted.

"Give me some ice-cream with the spoon, it will melt," Sonam said as she was dabbing the paint on canvas.

While RV fed Sonam and himself, he also painted. He brushed his eyelashes over her face to take pearl white, orangish red and painted on the canvas of his heart. For copperish orange, he used his eyelashes to brush out some from her amber eyes and a dash of green too.

"Give me the last bite RV, and take a look at the painting." RV had to bring his eyelashes back.

RV kissed her forehead and said, "It is perfect."

She wrote Sonam as an artist signature and told RV, "You also sign."

"Why?" RV asked.

"You fed me while I painted." She looked deep into his eyes and said, "These are the colours I got by spending a wonderful time with you, so you sign."

RV did not, could not say anything as her eyes said so much and he wrote RV below Sonam. Now what about the painting in RV's heart? Well! That cannot be signed as that will take at least a lifetime to paint.

10

The truck gang gave a flip of Latin and Punjabi music, leaving the atmosphere at the fort clicking its fingers.

It was their sixth day at Deogarh Fort when RV showed a photo of a resort to the gang. "Let's go there," everyone said together. RV sent a mail to Udaipur manager, telling him about the concept of their music holiday.

The Udaipur resort manager had agreed to host their truck gang and to let them play music at the resort for some days. They said bye to Rohan and started off that evening. There is something about long drives that weave a comfort cocoon.

After having dinner at the highway dhaba, they were enjoying their stupor induced by the dinner and highway breeze, except for Veer who was driving. Fairy lights of the truck were off. Aditi and Sonam shared a thick bedsheet, leaned their back on cushions against the truck body while their own bodies slipped more towards the mattress. RV and Shiv sat just opposite to them, more or less in the same position. As RV woke to pull the bedsheet, he saw something blinking. On his little lift of the head he could see many small blinks of light.

"Are we in the sky or the stars planned to come for a stroll on earth?" RV flapped his eyes to come out of his stupor and he realized they were glow worms, lakhs of them winking a few yards away. "Shiv, get up!" RV said shaking his shoulders. Aditi and Sonam were up with the sound and all of them stood up watching this sight. Veer also saw and he stopped the truck. There is no point hurrying through the journey when you miss so many things not lived on the way. The truck band let their hearts and eyes flicker with the glow worms.

"Sonam, you are the real rockstar and because of you, we became a truck band," Aditi said as she hugged her. Her look across Aditi's shoulder told RV, 'It is all because of you.'

'You are adorable,'RV's eyes answered back. She fell in love with herself.

RV drove the truck while Sonam sat with him. When RV pushed his hand at the gear, his well-toned muscles got ready to take command of the heavy truck. The way he was suited for an Audi or a Bullet, he suited for the truck too – a rare combination. The canopy of the trees stood like a guard at the king's palace and the spears of the guard kept opening as they approached the trees. Sonam kept looking out into the dark looking for swarm of glow worms.

Her phone beamed a message from her father, *"Come for this Himalayan retreat camp at Gangotri."* She read it and looked out. She could only see darkness and giants standing on both sides of the road to devour the truck.

"Sonam, talk to me, otherwise I might fall asleep." RV found this silence deafening. "Sonam, did you sleep?" RV said keeping his hand in hers.

She pulled her hand with a jerk. RV's heart sank and he slowed the truck. "RV, please find me a job here. I don't want to go anywhere for two months." She said in a high tone trying to suppress the voices of ashram bhajans, aarti, meditation, the dicipline of the ashram in the name of detoxification.

'Meditation can be done with natural beauty, things that you like. God didn't send us to do boring things. We are the creation of god. We need to celebrate the life given to us by him. Then only god will be happy,' Sonam spoke to herself, but did not say it aloud. She could speak to him about anything on earth, but didn't want to relive the whole thing as they discussed. She was also scared, 'What if he did not agree and had a different take on it?'

'Boring life... she had said that before also. If I ask her, she will feel the pain and might bleed out.' While Sonam indulged in mental dialogue, RV too thought hard to the point of hurting and then shelved the idea to ask and thought of just cheering her up.

"Yes Sonam, this fun we are having in the truck as a truck band, we will try to make it as our summer job to start with."

Sonam gave RV a quick hug, not disturbing his drive. She took out her phone and typed "*NO*" in capitals and sent it. Her parents were too involved with the camp to pester her more, so she could chill.

Sonam popped her head out of the window, banged hard on the truck body and shouted, "What's up guys!" She said it to the truck, the truck band and to herself. She had taken charge of her life and she had decided she would never let it become boring. She will do what gives her joy. RV honked the horn rhythmically to answer Sonam.

"Why can't our truck be parked at the pool side?" Sonam asked disappointed as she sat on the deck of the pool in her swimming costume and a sarong with her legs in water and her truck gang with her.

"I feel bad too, poor thing parked far away in the parking," Aditi said sitting on one of the loungers.

"Truck can be parked near the pool," Shiv said in a tone which had the power of a statement.

"The truck can enjoy a splash as well in the pool," RV said picking up the trial. Everyone had reached a bond. Everyone understood and they pulled on some clothes and were off in their truck. All of them were in jeans, was it the dress code of the place they were going to? No, the place was as spirited as the truck band. It attracted spontaneity. The place was the shallow pond, good old Chaparh, the place which had been the inspiration of swimming pool. But the original is always original.

They were going down the slope of a hillock when they all shouted. "There is our swimming pool." In the five voices there was a voice of the truck as well which chugged down the slope. The pond looked as if the artist had dropped an oil paint of white with shades of blue, giving it that freedom to spread wherever it wanted.

The gang started to splash water over the half immersed truck which was the only one in swimming costume as all its things had been kept in the rooms. Sonam curled her toes to dig in the mud, well nourished by the pond, letting them decide how to dig. Her ears caught swoosh of the water which rose when Aditi ran fast just for the sake of a swoosh. Sonam ran to join her to increase the volume of that swoosh. The boys cleaned the inside of the truck with buckets of water. They swam in the pond. Cluster of grass grew enjoying at the deck of the pond. The shrubs just lazed around, sun bathing. The truck band came out of the pond as every muscle of their body felt stretched and satisfied. After admiring their clean truck, they leaned against the tyres to relax as the truck shaded them. The humble Aravallis were a part of the bigger canvas of the artist and now the artist decided to include the truck and its gang in its painting.

The board read "Pool closed" but the pool side was alive with the music. The management had agreed to their idea of band in the truck. They would take a few guests in the truck to nearby places where they could play the music, listen, dance or whatever the guests where comfortable doing. The management was very happy with their innovative idea and yes, this indeed was their summer job for a month. Today it was only the truck gang playing the music for a few really interested guests. Music played at the swimming pool, which was held by two hillocks as it looked up at the rooms which had climbed to the different levels of the hillock. Sonam was still lighting the candles placed in clusters at different levels around the pool. Sonam bent to light, just a little bent as the height of the candle was four feet.

RV pressed the strings of the guitar but the music went and played at Sonam's pretty lips. Her lips shimmered in reddish maroon lipstick against the glow of the candle.

"Aditi, you play this!" RV gave the guitar and walked towards Sonam passing many such lit candles. RV slid his hand from the back of her waist. She looked into his eyes, but the sliding of his hand had conveyed everything. So the eyes saw only what the touch had given to them – all heat of passion and love.

The music started very Latin, the beats got inside them, wanting them to live only for that night. Their hands held the nape of each other's neck. The beats changed, and Sonam took RV's hand and slid back into the music. He held her waist and spinned it. Her flared skirt flirted with the music, enjoying every bit of it. This flirting put the music on a high note with a few drums. RV pulled her close with a hard stab on her back. She hit him, then turned to the front, both moving side, back, front... in rhythm.

Shiv sang a Latin American number, his voice mingling with the feeling of the lyrics. The guitar, the tango, the drums all gave music, on which the song would spread on people here who either danced or played music. They did whatever they did as if their life depended on it.

RV and Sonam's forehead rested on each other's as their bodies felt the rhythm and their hands went up to celebrate. The lips were close, very close. The music jumped up in jubilation and the drum beats became deeper. In response, Sonam's foot slid up the leg and she fell back clasping RV's hand. The blue sky above looked with envy at the blue waters of the swimming pool, which was the venue for today's night in celebration. Everything here was absorbed in itself, including the grass which grew around discovering life. RV again tugged at her waist towards him. This time the lips also fell on each other's lips. The lips met in quick 2-3 thuds. RV gathered her in his arms and the only place for her arms was RV's shoulders while their lips tasted the rythym of music, love, passion, the taste which they had not tasted before. The kiss splashed something enchanting inside their bodies. While dancing they had come far from the deck where only music reached. They were near the steps, which took to the rooms just like this kiss, which could take them to a cosy relationship if they decided to climb. RV's hand pressed against her silk off shoulder top which fell carelessly over her skirt clasped tight at the waist. The blue of the sky mixed with the blue water of the pool to give that blue to her top. The lips parted with a promise to meet again.

Sonam brought her hands down from his shoulders and buried her face in his chest, while RV's arms would not let go of her, even with a promise. RV's arm extended, Sonam rolled over it, keeping her arm over his, moved like the seconds' needle answering the music, mixing their shriek of joy through their dance. The music rotated with Sonam's waist, down in soft circular moves. The arms too let go of each other's arms as they danced as if there will be no tomorrow, but there was a beautiful bright tomorrow in their lives.

11

A cute little bench sat at the edge of the hillock where it could talk directly to the rising sun. Angelic Sonam sat in the bench after walking around the resort for some time. She enjoyed observing how the landscape of the place changed colours as it approached sunrise. The smile of the flowers, grass became brighter and brighter when their hearts danced at the thought of sunrise. Sonam's white dress reflected the orange along with the sky. Her hair fell, over the smocking part of the dress. The sun rose lighting up a tear drop which fell just near her thin straps like a pearl.

"Hey Angel," RV said as he cupped her face from behind. "You are crying?" RV asked as he felt his hands getting wet.

"Don't see the sun which is making you cry," and he took off his blue cap and made Sonam wear it, pushing the rim down. He felt like stopping the sun from rising if that was what made her cry and he was sure he could set down anything else responsible.

"Good you came RV," as she looked up forcing to see from under the cap. "I have never seen such a sunrise," Sonam said.

"Don't worry Sonam, I'll send a few clouds to cover it if that is what makes you cry."

She chuckled, which struck a few sparkles over her wet face. "I am so happy and don't know if what I am thinking is right or if I have the right to think that. I am impulsive, immature. I can't take decisions. I came for a rocking holiday. I have got one. The dance, the kiss has touched something deep, rocked the corners of my heart, which I never knew existed. I am not able to figure out what it is. Is it for real?"

RV took off her cap and said, "Look at the sunrise, the sky has figured out its true blue. See the grass and the wild flowers blushing, swaying on the rise of the slope. They are all learning to figure out. Don't worry, you will also figure out. The landscape around us is enjoying figuring out what the day will bring to them. Enjoy understanding the corners of your heart which you just discovered." He slid closer to her, putting his arm over her shoulders, disturbing the grass which creeped over his jeans. Both sat there seeing the sunrise till it urged them to get up with its hot rays.

RV got a garden pipe from the gardener who was watering the plants to wash away Sonam's tears. Sonam held her hair to bring her face close to the pipe which RV was holding. She moved her face over it, letting herself go with the flow.

"We are going to discuss something thrilling over breakfast today," RV told Sonam as they walked down the steps embeded in the hillock, where grass, rocks, wild flowers gave them company. They were now passing by the pool and could taste the kiss, but they decided to taste the breakfast. This place had slipped down from the Aravallis and the coffee colour tables were crowned with fawn umbrellas.

"RV, tell me about your exciting plan."

"Let everyone else come."

"I am dying with the suspense," Sonam said.

"I too died seeing your tears. Now it is my turn to trouble you." They sat on the chairs across the table, facing each other.

"Okay guess," RV said.

"Going to another pond?" Sonam asked.

"No," RV said enjoying Sonam's restlessness.

"Singing Rajasthani Songs," Sonam guessed again.

"Try better!"

She went on with her wild guesses and now the truck band was complete on the table.

RV declared, "We will paint our truck with spray paint."

Sonam and Aditi played their tabla of delight on the table.

"And there is more… the management has approved the idea of a carnival with our truck for this resort."

Sonam and Aditi now stood up on the chairs to do a quick jig of exuberance. The people sitting around just got a little teaser of what was going to engulf them.

They were in a big old haveli which had airs of royalty as it danced in various types of fabrics, sarees, paintings and artefacts. They had already bought the spray paints and paint bombs but the streets of Udaipur would not let them go. They scattered seeing the things of their interest at the haveli as their eyes scooped out carvings and mirrors.

"See RV, isn't this amazing!" Shiv showed him a knife with a carved silver cover. As RV pulled out the knife, his eyes were pulled to the opposite end of the haveli by the swirl of a colourful hand-crafted mirror skirt which Sonam wore on top of her dress, swirling, enjoying herself, and showing Aditi too.

"RV, this is a great piece," Shiv said.

"Yes it is," RV said giving back the knife and still looking at Sonam.

'Oh! Sonam looks like a Goddess Bohemian with these silver chains on her head' and RV imagined himself bending down to kiss her forehead.

"You buy this blue and I will buy the red one," Aditi told Sonam

"Look at these glass candle stands," Aditi got one blue and one green. "I will also buy for my house," Aditi said.

"You want some, RV?"

"No, my mom gets crystal from Europe. I don't think she would like to keep this."

"Sonam might want to buy," RV said.

"No, I don't want to increase the luggage and we get this in Delhi."

In reality, she knew this gift won't be appreciated when most of the time her parents were away for some meditation camps and even at home they were busy with kirtan mandlis. She broke her thoughts, engaging them to the colourful lanterns.

They walked the lanes of this bazaar which had a certain character due to a history of many centuries. No mall in the world can ever have such a character. They walked, stopped at any shop that held their interest and struck a conversation with the shopkeepers. They bought a mirror frame in thikri work for their carnival.

"Both of you should have dinner at the Laxmi Palace," Aditi told RV and Sonam.

"You all also come, it will be fun," Sonam said.

"No Sonam, we have been there many times. I want to sleep." Aditi yawned, making clear what she had said.

"RV, we will take this frame. I want to see IPL sitting on my bed," Shiv said.

"Me too," Veer said.

"Okay, see you tomorrow, bye." RV and Sonam said.

The palace was quite near and soon RV and Sonam's taxi was climbing the road which was taking them to the orangish yellow painted mahal. They got down and walked on this green lawn while the Fateh Sagar Lake walked towards them. The sun rays rowed evening mood in the lake and the beauty of the mahal made the rays tipsy. There was a competition. Who was tipsier, the rays or RV and Sonam in each other's untold love. RV slid his hand behind Sonam's waist while they looked down at the huge lawn of the mahal. The lake yearned to kiss the lawn, but the confusion of the world ran between them. The band started to play at the lawns, creating music, perhaps to blow a flying kiss for the lake which sat cordorned with its banks. But Sonam's heart enjoyed as RV's love was cardoning her heart, but the cordon was not complete yet. The blushing light of the sun hopped on to the lights of the Udaipur city, not just The Lalit Mahal.

"The band can be a part of the carnival," Sonam said, sitting at one of the tables at the lawns.

"Yes, come, we will go talk to them now."

The band people were already coming up when they got up. "Bhaiya, we are having a grand carnival at the resort. Can you play there or someone else as good as you can play for our carnival? Please, please?" Sonam went on.

RV already was part of this carnival which was evident on Sonam's face. "We have a band for our carnival," RV and Sonam said to each other, breaking into quick claps.

They sat on their table when the waiter came and said, "Sir, we have a special whisky on the menu today. Would you like to order?"

"No, thank you! I am fine with a fresh orange juice," RV said.

"And what about the lady?" the waiter asked Sonam.

"I will also be fine with an orange juice."

"The waiter is conspiring that I again get drunk and you will get all the adventure of taking me home. I mean, the resort."

"You mean that day at the Amer Palace, I enjoyed the adventure?" Sonam said looking at RV. "Ya, actually it was quite an adventure, climbing the hillock, getting you down, in the car," Sonam said remembering the night.

"While I was oblivious to all the fun that you were having at my cost," RV continued.

"RV, you have some tequila shots. It will be fun. That day I did not know anyone. Here I can call Shiv, Veer and Aditi."

"No, no why give them the trouble, these pretty girls at the hotel will help you," RV said. "I think I will order tequila shots because I can also see some good looking guys around; they will help you take me and this time you enjoy the fun."

He cupped her face across the table in his hands, looking into her eyes, doing most of the talking, but the words also poured in a bit saying, "We want to enjoy each other in full senses, our company gives an un-matchable high."

RV's cell phone rang and he had to pull his hand to answer the cell-phone. "Hi Mom, how is Belgium and our diamonds.

That's like my Mom. No mom I can't come. You know I don't like these exhibitions, even if it is special with the royal family. I am doing a fun summer job. Understand Mom. Tell Dad too. Bye Mom. Love you."

RV got restless after the call and told Sonam, "My mom and dad look for high profile customers, preferably from a royal family to sell their pieces of diamond. They throw lavish parties and try to get them featured in magazines, mentioning it is designed by them."

"And they want you to come," Sonam completed.

"Yes, they have been trying from many years. I have been to a few, but I hate it." They had almost finished their dinner and RV immediately asked for their check.

"We will walk down," Sonam suggested thinking that the late night breeze would sooth his nerves. Sonam twined both her arms on RV's arm, while leaning over the arm like a vine entwines a pole. Yes, a pole. RV's senses became quite like the pole who would not feel the tenderness and embrace of her arms.

"Taxi!" RV called out, but the taxi did not stop. The city looked quite rested in its night avatar. But RV did not feel rested as he shouted a few abuses when the taxi did not slop.

"RV, don't bother, there is another one coming."

"Stop stop, we want to go to this resort."

And before RV was through telling the place to the driver, the driver said, "No sorry, I can't go that far."

"You son of a bitch, come out!" RV plucked open the door and pulled him out. "You cannot refuse to go."

"Who are you? I will refuse. What can you do?" The driver showed an attitude and thrust his hand on RV's chest.

"Okay, you will not drive? Then you sit, I will drive," RV slapped him hard with the sound vibrating in the still night. "Just sit on the other seat," RV took out the keys. The driver was a short guy and when he saw the quiver of muscles in RV's broad shoulders, he sat quiety after briefly looking at RV's eyes which were spitting fire. The driver sat in the passenger seat, while RV drove fast, being familiar to the roads helped him navigate his way.

Sonam was pleasantly surprised, though her face was bewildered trying to join pieces of the happenings to make out something coherent. "Now you understand... never let customers walk on the roads late night and helpless, people need to go to hospitals, girls need to get home." RV told the taxi driver after getting down and gave him a tip along with the fare.

"Understood, sir," the taxi wala said, understanding his mistake and saluted RV too.

Sonam also wanted to Salute RV, but RV said a quick good night before going to his room as he suddenly realized that Sonam had seen his anger, a new RV, and she might not like it.

'What did I do! I could have found another taxi. This might confuse Sonam.' RV lay in his bed with all kinds of disturbing thoughts and slept dreaming of being lost in mist on some hills.

12

Shiv, Sonam and the whole gang had started having breakfast under the beige umbrella when RV walked with ruffled hair in blue jeans and a round neck T-shirt. He had woken up only after everyone had called many times.

"Sonam and I have engaged one band too, which can be a part of our carnival." RV picked up a toast and applied butter to it.

Shiv took a sip of his sweet lime juice and said, "We should create some excitement about the carnival here at the resort."

"Let's make colourful posters," Sonam suggested.

"We should finish painting them before we start painting the bus," Veer added.

"Wait Aditi, I am also coming for a refill," Sonam joined Aditi on the buffet table topping up the conversation with carnival.

"Try these blue berry cakes," Aditi said as she kept one on Sonam's plate.

Sonam felt the softness of the cake seep in her mouth.

RV's room soon turned into an artist's studio with paints and paint pallettes everywhere. Sonam bent down over the chart paper with the pencil behind her ear and hair held in a bun.

She drew their truck over it. 'TRUCK CARNIVAL' read in bold on the chart paper. 'The Carinval of life – Age no bar. '

'THIS CARNIVAL will introduce you to YOURSELF

TURN HOLIDAY SPIRIT INTO CARNIVAL OF LIFE MUSIC, BAND, DANCE, TATOO, SINGING – LIFE IS A CARNIVAL' was written on various chart papers.

"We need a tatoo artist," Shiv said.

"Manager is arranging one," replied Veer.

Sonam was leaning against the wall with the pencil still behind her ear, looking out of the window. "Why don't we get flower tiaras made." Her gaze brought up this idea after touching the flowers of the resort.

"Blooming idea," Veer remarked.

"Yes, these gardeners will make beautiful tiaras," RV said looking at some of the gardeners watering plants.

They rolled the ready chart papers, all decked up to blow the conch of the carnival. Sonam held one chart paper over her eye and through the tunnel of this paper she could see RV's eye shooting a bullet through this paper canon. Sonam brought down the chart as her blood was being churned by the bullet into something lethally sweet.

RV and Sonam walked on the stairs cut on the slope of the hillock. They were going to put the charts in the club house which was two levels above their room.

"Put some by the swimming pool too," Sonam shouted telling Veer who was already on his way down.

Aditi and Shiv had gone to stir the restaurant with this excitement.

"Meet us for lunch," Veer shouted back.

It was noon, with the sun reigning supreme. But romance has its own throne, who-so-ever's reign it might be. RV saw Sonam's face turn red and hot. He spotted a banana tree and pulled out a leaf and held it parallel over their head. Sonam's eyes glided over the smooth green surface of the leaf, occassionally enjoying the bounce over the edges which cascaded down in graceful slopes. RV's eyes were busy picking up filtered green light over Sonam's flushed face. The embers of romance were fanned by this leaf. It was a wonder why the leaf still remained green and did not turn brown.

They entered the club house. "Hi kids! What's up!" RV and Sonam greeted the kids who played table tennis and carom. They kept the leaf on the chair and started to pin up the chart paper on the notice board.

"What is this?" some kids gathered around them.

"There is a carnival tomorrow," RV said.

"Here at the resort?" Some kids asked, not hiding their excitement.

"Wow, a carnival," cute litte girl said.

"Can we get our footballs too?" boys asked.

"Of course, it is just fun! Get whatever you like to walk with," RV replied.

"There is music, dance, you can play guitar, hop on and off the truck too," Sonam said, equally excited as the kids.

"I can't wait for tomorrow," a girl with two plaits said.

"Me too," replied Sonam.

"My list of can't wait things is increasing every moment," RV said to himself.

Sonam had tied a mustard and blue silk scarf around her head and wore blue Ray-Bans. She held a blue spray paint bottle in her hand. Her hair fell in the front, covering most of her neck.

RV was busy writing on the side body of the truck with chalk. He wrote – TRUCKS AND TRUCKS OF LOVE, MUSIC, DANCE, FUN! When he turned to take paint, his heart felt wrapped in colour by Sonam's look. The truck gang indulged in good three hours of painting. Sonam's white T-shirt got sprayed in different colours. They painted some guitars and drums too. But the image it had of running on the highway was not touched.

"We will discuss a few things for tomorrow with the manager," Shiv and Veer said.

"I will go to the room and relax! Probably watch a movie," Aditi streched her back.

"I want to go for a walk," Sonam said as she got an invitation from white mogra lined road leading out of the resort.

"RV, please be my escort, otherwise I will get lost," Sonam looked at RV without the Ray-Bans and with the scarf still on her head.

"You mean I am your GPS?" RV said.

"Bye GPS and Sonam... see you for dinner at ten," Aditi called out.

"Bye, we will be back by then," Sonam said looking back and then took two-three quick steps to fall in step with RV.

"What were you saying RV? GPS! Actually you have acted like GPS for me. I was not able to find a way out of my boring life and you positioned my life."

The jasmine flowers of the bushes on both sides of the road moved their way out of the leaves, restless to take a glimpse of the moon. Their affair with the night was being spoken through the fragrance. Sonam bent over the jasmine bush to gather a few flowers while RV's eyes spread over her truck tattoo. RV prisoned his hands in his pockets as he did not want to disrupt the walk so soon.

She stopped near a thorny bush and spread her folded hands to admire her collected joy. RV plucked a thorn from the bush took a flower from her hand and he sew the flower to her white T-shirt with the thorn. He plucked another thorn and used it like a pin to hold the flower on the T-shirt. He took all care to sew the thorn into the T-shirt without pricking her skin, not realizing that the brush of his fingers were pricking her skin with poisonous passion. The only antidote for this poison was RV's touch. RV was committing sorcery and she was possessed.

"Hello!" RV tried to talk to her possessed soul as he blew over her eyelashes."All the flowers have been fixed to your T-shirt."

Sonam lowered her eyelashes, lifted them again to say, "This kind of dress has never been made before." The sorcerer was getting overpowered by the soul, but he continued with his sorcery.

"I have something to boast all my life that I have the best designer dress in the world."

"Why Sonam, is this the last time we are walking together? It can be another walk with another designer dress," RV said as he walked with his hands back in his pocket.

"So, you are a genius who has no dearth of innovative stuff." Sonam teased, trying to take the discussion away about the walk in future as she had not thought, rather was scared of thinking about the future.

"I am not a genius, but an admirer, and when I look at you, even in thoughts, innovative ideas hit me."

She could now feel the moonlight seeping into her skin, bringing with it the tenderness and softness of jasmine flowers.

"You, you are a flirt," Sonam said as she stepped on to a rock just for a little adventure that this rock offered on this straight road.

"I can flirt more," RV said and kissed her on the tatoo which was exposed as her hair fell in front. This soft kiss hit her like a jolt and she fell back into RV's arms. RV turned her, looked at her face washed with moonlight. He tried to rub moonlight from her lips to his. Sonam's eyes closed, offering themselves. RV's lips shifted there to rub. He kissed her forehead before engulfing her in his arms.

Sonam tried to loosen the grip. "What happened?" RV asked confused and scared with her behaviour.

"If you hug me too tight, the flowers on my top will get spoilt," Sonam said as she checked if her flowers got spoilt. A naughty smile danced on his lips and before Sonam realized what was happening, RV linked his arms with hers from her back and lifted her with her back on his back.

"This is truly another innovative master stroke. Please RV, don't put me down, take me like this till the other turn." At the turn on the road, she slipped down and she enjoyed this also. It is this romance which would show them the road to love.

13

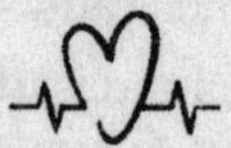

"Trucks and trucks of love" stood sprayed in orange when the evening rays fell over it. The truck stood enjoying the band which played on this huge parking area. Shiv, Veer and RV gave tiaras to all the girls who came for the carnival. Tatoo artists made tattoos for whoever wanted. The truck band people were able to induce the spirit of the carnival during the marketing of this fun procession.

Girls of all age groups felt like princess wearing tiaras.

Some kids walked with the band, matching their steps, and some tried to play the instruments of the band through action, but the effect got doubled.

The band went quiet and when everybody looked around to know why it was quiet, they saw RV on the bonnet of the truck, blowing the trumpet. As he held the golden instrument, his arm muscles made a statement revealed by the black vest he wore over his ripped jeans. Sonam whistled a lot of oomph in her red off-shoulder flared frock and her long angel sleeves added another wave of music to this musical journey.

Aditi and Sonam climbed on the bonnet. Shiv started to play the guitar standing on the crown of the truck. Veer started playing drums sitting inside the truck. The truck band started singing a rocking number.

One of the drivers of the resort drove the truck and the musical carnival started going up the gradient of the resort as well in the excitement. It was that perfect evening time when the sun blows its good bye kiss for the day. RV helped a few kids to come inside the truck. Veer was already settled on the wooden box to play the bongo drum.

"Give me these cowbells! I can play them," a guy in his twenties told RV. RV gave him the bells, feeling glad that they found another musician to add on. Well! He was able to find five more musicians in the crowd whom he distributed various instruments to. The band people also got a carnival makeover and they either borrowed from RV or shared their instrument. RV and Aditi joined Shiv in the crowd and sang rocking songs. The band people, the truck people and the frenzy of others were the waves of this musical sea which then hit the shores of this resort, bringing it to life.

Small boys danced with so much enthusiasm that the thud of their feet already travelled to the second level of the hillock. The young people rocked while the older lot skipped and swayed. The staff of the resort took various positions on the hillock to clap and wave to the carnival. Their mania made another wave of this musical sea.

The truck stopped completely now. Aditi, Sonam and RV sat on the bonnet and some other people also hopped on to the bonnet. They sat on the bonnet with their legs sloping down while the hands went up in claps, swaying… The truck started to move, but the pace of the truck still allowed them to sit on the bonnet. The fairy lights of the truck glowed in competition with the music as it was dark now. The garden lights, resort lights… travelled like ships in the sea of this music.

The truck gang belted out hit music from across the world, singing together, sometimes coming down to sing and dance with other people. As Sonam gave the mike to kids who sat on the bonnet, they leaned all around her to sing along. Sonam gave the kids the mike and she got up to sway her hands up along with RV.

This carnival and its zeal now reached the table land at the fifth level. The truck stood under silver flags tied on thin LED wires which shaded the whole area where the carnival was to party in its celebration. The thikri glass frame was fixed in one corner and people photographed themselves in this frame. The kids climbed up and down the truck. Music and singing went on, mike exchanged hands from kids to teens to adults. And they bared themselves without being judged.

The gang was having paneer tikka from the barbeque, quite hungry after the games with kids. The barbeque chief made whatever anyone wanted and even let people barbeque.

"Shiv will barbecue for us," Aditi said.

"Our Shiv makes mind blowing stuff, especially in vegetarian," Veer endorsed.

"Dude, you are trapped," RV teased.

"Only on one condition… everyone will have to eat whatever I make." Shiv took the stuff from the chief and started adding spices, marinating.

"This is last now, Shiv. I can't have anymore," Sonam said taking a deep breath, trying to make place for the extra she had eaten. "I want to take a walk, and yes yes, I want to lie in the hammock at the other end of the resort."

"RV can accompany you; we want to eat more," Veer and shiv said together and Aditi nooded.

"We will go down this road, then climb the other hillock. I have seen a hammock somewhere there from my room window. This much of walk is needed to make myself feel light," Sonam said as they walked down the slope of the road. RV's hand slipped over her waist which fitted so well, like it belonged there.

"Your waist will also say thank you after the walk, it is carrying the weight of the food."

Sonam stopped after walking downhill, turned to look at RV, and said at her impulsive best, "Actually yes, you are right. This little downhill walk has helped; now let's give my waist a little rest. So you and my digestive juices help my waist, carry me on your back till the first level of this hillock." Sonam already stood on the little chunk of the side wall to take advantage of its height.

RV held her hands to keep on his shoulders and she smoothly slipped over his back. His arms cupped her legs and her arms circled his neck while he climbed up the gradual gradient. "RV, you could be a very good mountaineer. You will be very nicely able to carry everything in a rucksack."

"Yes, my rucksack will talk also, keep me amused in my adventures," RV replied as he adjusted his hands and bent a little to make her grip better.

"Enough of the speaking rucksack RV, we will try mountaineering together. Enough practice for you. I am coming down now."

RV stretched his body and said, "Better would be I try carrying gunny bags of flour. That way I will earn something."

"Brilliant idea, and with the money that you earn, we will buy our truck."

Sonam had hardly finished saying this when both looked at each other and excitement of their tone resonated together, "Buy our truck!"

"This truck is family now. I don't want to think how, but I always want this truck," Sonam said while they had reached that part of the hillock where the stars whispered something to the hillock.

"Sonam, we can make our own resort somewhere, something on a smaller scale with our truck. We can make people enjoy in a different kind of holiday. Music, of course, will be a major part."

"We can put easles in exquisite places and they can paint. They can try pottery; try a hand on music instruments," Sonam continued almost jumping with excitement.

"We will go for jungle and field music shows," RV said and this time the romance of the plan made him keep his arm on her shoulders.

"Then we can take the tourists to that pond where they can swim and wash the truck," Sonam said.

"Those hammocks should be here," Sonam said when she saw this open area after the rooms overlooking the outline of other hillocks. "But I can't see any now." Sonam went around in the dark searching for them frantically. She was also looking for ways to fulfill the dreams they had just weaved together.

RV also searched for any hammock there as he hugged their dreams tighter, feeling scared lest uncertainties do not snatch them away. RV didn't want to ask Sonam if she had figured out her feelings for him, after he had seen her cry on the bench. He wanted her to feel her heart, his heart, what this holiday was saying to her. RV's heart also sank when he could not find the hammock.

"Are you sure this was the place?" he asked.

"Yes, see that is my room on the other hillock, and from the window, you can see this place only." Sonam pointed to her room window.

"Never mind Sonam, we will come again in the morning."

"Ok, let's walk till the edge and see the valley down." As they walked towards the edge, their feet got entangled in something.

"Here it is," they said. The hammock was there on the ground, blown by the wind. New energy was infused in their thought process. They picked it up. "RV, let's tie the hammock to these trees here," Sonam said while they were getting it near the trees.

"Sonam, you just hold the hammock, I will tie."

RV hurled Sonam in the hammock so that she feels the little bounce. RV also hopped on to the hammock and sat in an inclined position opposite to her.

"Sonam, we will put a couple of these at our truck adda at the top of the mountain," RV tried to move his feet away as they almost reached her waist.

"I don't mind feet, if they don't smell," Sonam joked.

RV brought his feet back, almost touching her arm and waist as he said, "And your feet are asking for a massage." RV started rubbing under her feet and she realized that her feet were really tired after the dancing and games. They felt cradled by the mountains lit up at a few places, enjoying the breeze.

RV lightly pressed her toes, then caressing with upward strokes till the ankle. The soothing effect caressed her eyelashes and her eyes closed. Love is not always passion; it is outrageously soothing too. The feeling of soft delicate feet in his hands and the satisfaction of making her feel rested put RV to sleep.

14

Sonam felt water drops on her eyes and lips; she could see it in her dreams. A big drop of water fell on her eyes and water seeped inside. She opened her eyes, looking into the dark blue veil of the sky. The veil was becoming heavy with rain and turning grey. Everything around her was still asleep, including RV, as it was early dawn.

'We slept here in the hammock and these are actual rain drops. I wasn't dreaming.' The thrill of sleeping in a hammock under open skies and waking up in rain wanted to make her scream, but she restrained. Instead, she started to tickle under RV's feet just next to her hand.

Within a few seconds of tickling, RV woke up and said, "I gave you a soothing foot massage and this is what you do to my feet," RV said straightening his back against the hammock.

"This was my way of foot massage and RV, would you want to miss this dawn in rain sleeping?" It was then that RV realized the drops falling.

"I want to enjoy the rain falling over me for a long time." Sonam said, making herself more comfortable in the hammock.

"Look there at the hillocks, the shrubs and trees, they are simmering in a grayish blush, waiting to be throbbed by air," Sonam said. RV looked at the hillocks and beyond, feeling the freshness of everything. These things always existed, but it was RV and Sonam's love which was actually showing everything to them now.

When RV's eyes returned, they saw the rain dancing on her face. Suddenly, lightning lit the sky with lyrics and thunder started beating the drums. Sonam jumped down from the hammock with RV. The rain became very heavy, filling puddles, giving them opportunity to jump and splash.

"Let's go to the restaurant and have hot tea. It is almost six. I think we might find the cook there," RV said. They walked till the restaurant, letting rain do the talking.

"Excuse me, can we get hot tea, preferably with ginger?" Sonam asked the person who was going in the kitchen while they sat under the umbrella.

"I don't think you will get at this time," he replied.

"You are making so much for breakfast; just boiling tea won't take long," RV told him.

"No, not possible," the cook told them in a rude tone.

"You are making tea now and with ginger! We are guests here and also work here. Anyway, that is none of your business; you just make tea," RV's eyes turned red.

"I will not do what you want." The cook was quite adamant and stood with his hands on his waist.

RV got up with one thrust and started pushing the cook while saying, "You will not make tea?"

"No!" the cook continued and he too tried to push RV, but RV was too tall and strong for him.

Sonam tried to pacify the cook and said, "Bhaiya, let's go inside the kitchen."

"I will get you fired," and RV started to dial the manager's number.

Sonam was able to pacify the cook and she took him inside. "Bhaiya, I understand you are busy, let me make some tea myself. I am part of the staff, not a guest. Please."

Sonam's friendly humble approach sucked the Cook's anger. "Okay! I will make tea, and you go drive some sense into that tall guy," the cook said and finally smiled.

"Just don't worry; he won't say anything to the Manager. Just make tea, and let me come and take it."

"Yes ma'am, in two minutes."

"The manager's phone is out of coverage area," RV said looking at his phone still frowning.

Sonam took the phone away from his hand and said, "No need! He is making tea." RV's frown line smoothened as he looked at Sonam.

Sonam lay in her soft bed with her back resting on the pillows. She felt cosy and nice after a hot water bath. The bed had been so inviting after so many hours in the rain. And the blanket with which she had covered herself wrapped her in warmth. Although most of the cosy warmth she felt was provided by RV's love, the blanket was unnecessarily taking the credit. There was still time for their usual meeting at the club house or some place to discuss wonderful ideas to entertain the guests.

Just then, her room bell rang. She walked barefoot in her shorts and T-shirt with her hair still having streaks of water.

"Hi Aditi, come!"

"Sonam, I have decided we are going to spend all girl's day today," Aditi said as she sat on the bed dressed casually in shorts and T-shirt. Her short hair was tucked behind her ear in which single small diamond earrings blinked.

"I am calling up RV to tell him that both of us are not coming for the discussion," and she was already dialling his number.

"There is no reply. I will tell Shiv. "Hi Shiv, me and Sonam are having a girly time. You guys can decide what you want to do. Okay, bye." She hurled the phone away.

Aditi's phone rang again. "Yes my chooza. I will come after a month, you plan to come here with mom-dad, read some nice romantic novels. Tell me the story tomorrow. I am with Sonam and we plan to have a girly day." As Aditi kept the the phone down, Sonam tried to push back a wave of emptiness of a sibling.

"That was your sister's phone, show me her photograph," Sonam said.

"Sure," and aditi pulled her pillow next to Sonam's and showed photos to her."

"So cute… this in school uniform," Sonam got engrossed seeing the photos.

"Do you fight with her?"

"Of course! That is most important part of love. These days she discusses all her crushes with me."

"I don't have a brother or sister." Sonam just said it, which was so very Sonam who would not keep anything in her heart.

"I know it is bad, now with whom would you discuss your crush on RV?" Aditi's naughty eyes blew naughtiness towards Sonam, blowing out everything else. "Now sweetheart, you don't have any choice, as I am your only sister. You will have to discuss your crush with me. I know it is love, but I want to hear from the crush stage," and Aditi sat cross-legged on the bed.

'Sister, first make me a hot coffee," Sonam said still lying in her blanket, only with her head and neck popping out on the pillow.

"I think you guys were in the rain till late in the night," Aditi said as she switched on the kettle to boil water.

"Not late in the night, but the whole night. We came in the morning."

"Now that's like a good sister, telling me everything," as she raised her eyebrows at Sonam while she emptied sugar, coffee and milk sachets into two coffee mugs. "And you are getting this mug only if you tell me what you did in the night."

"Of course I am telling you what we did the whole night," Sonam said and extended her hand to take the hot coffee which was steaming just like her lips.

Aditi sat cross-legged, ready to hear and said, "Tell me from the beginning, first the last night. Sonam sipped her coffee sending stream of suspense as she sat opposite Aditi.

"We walked. No, a correction here; RV walked carrying me on his back like a rucksack."

"How romantic," Aditi said gripping the coffee mug with both hands.

"Then we reached the hammock and he put me in the hammock," Sonam continued.

"And then," Aditi asked.

"RV also lay down in the hammock, giving me foot massage."

Aditi now forgot about the coffee too.

"Then we slept." Sonam sipped her coffee.

"No wonder all the girls in our school had a crush on him. He was in twelfth standard when I was in tenth and my class girls were always after me to introduce them to him," Aditi told Sonam.

"Yes, my RV is like that," Sonam said as she wondered how she said my RV when neither he nor she had confessed their love. While Sonam sipped the last sip of coffee. Aditi noticed her nail paint.

"Sonam, you need to repaint your nails," Aditi said. She was already taking out remover and nail paints from her cute little sling bag. Aditi took the cup from her hand and pulled a chair near her. "Give me your hand. My sister loves it when I paint her nails." Aditi dipped the cotton in remover and started to remove the old nail paint. The remover took out the vacuum of a loving sister along with the nail paint. "Here are the paints I have. Which one do you want? You have such pretty fingers and toes, any colour will look good," Aditi said as she chose a shocking pink.

Sonam was cherishing every minute of it. "Keep your hands here. I will take a picture and send it to RV," Aditi said as she put the cap back on the nail polish.

Sonam posed with her freshly painted toes and nails and the photo was sent to RV. The photo just stayed unseen as RV didn't want to face his mood because of the way he had behaved with the cook and thinking Sonam might not like it. So he tried to drown it with sleep.

Sonam blew air over her nails and Aditi was filing hers. "Aditi, my nail paint has dried. I want to paint yours."

"OK!" Aditi kept her hands on the pillow which was on Sonam's legs. "Sonam, I don't feel like going for lunch at the restaurant. Order something here and tell me how you and RV met."

"Done," Sonam said as she finished painting her last nail. This is what friends are for, to paint each other in colours of fun and security. "This tatoo at your ankle is damn cute," Sonam said.

"But your tatoo is special."

"How?" Sonam asked

"Do you think we don't know? The cocks on the windscreen of your truck tattoo are in shape of RV and tattoo on RV's shoulder shows off the cocks as SS." Aditi said as she got up to admire Sonam's tattoo exposed by her razor back T-shirt. "This truck tatoo truly binds us," Aditi said feeling nostalgic.

"Please get two veg burgers, two french fries and two fresh lime sodas," Sonam told the room service over the phone looking at Aditi for the order's approval. Sonam drew the curtains apart and the whole wall which was in glass made the room effortlessly flow into the wild grass, the sky and mountains.

"Sonam, you are from Delhi. Delhi is such a hip and happening city."

"Yes, it is. But there is so much pollution and life is fast-paced. And a city has nothing much to do with a happening life. People can make their life enjoyable if they choose."

"True Sonam, with our friends, this music band of ours in Jaipur, we have a rocking time and then my mom, dad, and sister... we are one crazy family." Just then, the bell rang and Aditi collected their lunch order. Aditi placed the burgers on the glass table which provided enough height to the floor cushions.

"This is just the colour of the french fries which my mom makes," Aditi dipped a french fry in sauce as she made herself comfortable on the floor cushion.

Sonam was still circling the French fry in the sauce as various images of her mom going to meditation camps, kirtans, gurus, strict diets circled in her mind. She moved the French fries across the sauce and then back, cut the images and then took a bite, smiling. They moved the table away to spread their legs, resting their hands on soft cushions facing each other as Sonam told her how she met RV with Aditi adding on as she knew most of it. They discussed about everything under the sky. About the dresses, bad sense of style of many celebrities and how both of them could give them tips for better dressing.

"And the red carpet, it appears some science fiction characters are walking the carpet," Sonam said.

"Absolutely!" Aditi replied. The rays of the sun held on to the day at four, listening to this girly conversation.

"This must be our truck gang?" Sonam said as she got up from the floor cushion to answer the door bell.

"May we disturb the girl gang," Shiv asked.

"You may," Sonam said swinging her arm in gesture.

"Our truck band has got transferred to topi gang," Aditi commented as she saw them dressed in tracks and smart caps, still sitting on the floor cushion, now cross-legged.

"Yes, you both also join the topi gang; we are going cycling," Veer said leaning against the wall.

"Sonam, make coffee for everyone," Shiv said as he and RV were sitting on the chairs which almost made a circle with the floor cushions. RV looked at Sonam as she plugged the kettle.

RV's self-remorse about his behaviour slowly escaped like the steam from the nozzle of the kettle. RV thought that how could he ever create a tense situation.

Veer emptied the coffee and sugar sachets in red coffee mugs and Sonam poured the boiling water from the kettle.

"It is time to do cheers with coffee." Sonam stirred the contents. Veer gave the cups to everyone.

"Cheers!" They clinked the coffee mugs together and said, "To our rocking truck band!" RV took a sip and when the concoction of milk, sugar, friendship and love hit his head, he realized he could curb his anger and not let anything ugly crop up.

"Girls, get ready and come down. We are going at the reception to see if our cycles have been arranged," RV said.

Five cycles rode on the smooth road which had wings of fields, bushes, hillocks as far as the cyclists could see. The five o'clock sun gave them that extra dash of style with their blue, green Ray-Bans under their caps. The cylists took a turn now. As they rode further, a lake appeared and looked like a blue spot on the wings.

Sonam lifted her chin to enjoy the breeze which was on its way to spread evening. The cycles were on a slope, going down, so they stopped pedalling and enjoyed the journey with no worry or hurry to reach any destination.

"Wow! Sugarcane fields," Sonam stopped and the rest of them also found it interesting to stop. Sonam almost ran to pluck one.

"Take this!" RV offerred her one as she was still struggling to take it out. They were the easy to peal ones. RV sat on a milestone holding his sugarcane. He was about to take a bite when he saw Sonam peeling her sugarcane fast with that childlike sense of achievement, still standing inside the field. Sonam bit out a big chunk of sugarcane and chewed sucking in the juice. As Sonam was about to tear another chunk, her eye met RV's. She started walking towards him, jumping culvets to be with him.

"RV, you broke the sugarcane for me, now I will give you peeled chunks of sugarcane," and saying that, she dug her teeth into the sugarcane to take out an irregular blob of sugarcane. She offered it with a stem of sugarcane. RV chewed and wondered if anything ever could taste this intoxicating. "RV, you know, this is the first time I am eating sugarcane?"

"You never got a chance to be near a sugarcane field?" RV asked while chewing his sugarcane.

"I have been to a sugarcane field many times," Sonam said as the images of sugarcane fields with strict sewadars of ashram she visited with her parents as a kid splashed in her mind. "But you were not there to pull a soft one out for me," Sonam said chewing away her bad boring memories with the sugarcane and tasting the juice of her upbeat zippy life.

"Sonam, I have also not had this juicy sweet ones," he said, taking another candy like sugarcane from her.

"I am sure that you have not." She winked at him. "Oh! my god RV," Sonam said.

"What happened?"

"My wink was perfect. I finally got it. There was no forced twitching of the muscles. It was natural. Wasn't it, RV?"

"Ya.:. But..." RV was amused by her reaction.

"You know what, I have been practicing to wink in front of a mirror from so many years now."

"So ma'am, can you teach this rare art to me?"

"I will I will. Try to keep your left eye open and try to bring the eyelash of your right eye down with a little twitch of the right cheek muscle."

"Ok, here I go," and in the process he closed both his eyes.

"Not like this, RV. See how I wink, be very natural," and she winked very naturally. Now try again.

"I am sure I got it this time," and RV bangs his cheek into his right eye."

"No RV, not like this." Sonam kept on telling him the techniques in different ways and RV kept blinking in all kinds of funny ways.

"OK RV, now feel very naughty and then try to wink," and she winked more seductively this time. RV again twitched his right cheek hard. "Forget it RV, you need a lot of practice," and Sonam was back to chewing sugarcane. RV also picked up his own sugarcane and began to eat.

Aditi, Shiv and Veer went far deep into the fields. After eating, they were finding good ones to cut. "Why are you cutting extra?" Sonam cupped her mouth to double the effect of her shout.

"We will take some along," Shiv shouted back.

"Great idea, literally sweet one," she showed her thumbs up to them.

With sugarcanes tied with dried creepers cyclists were on their way back, sometimes two cycles riding little in the front and three at the back, or at times all five in a row together…

chatting. The traffic-free road offered them this liberty. The sun light had got cooked to orange.

"Aditi, I taught RV how to wink today. Can you wink?"

"No Sonam."

"Okay, I will teach you also. RV, tell Aditi how to wink,"as Sonam turned to tell RV this, she saw RV wink at Shiv and he winked back. It just took a few seconds for Sonam to understand that RV already knew how to wink. "I am not leaving you today," Sonam said and she started pedalling faster when RV started to take a lead, pedalling faster. RV stopped only after reaching the resort and she encountered him by bringing her cycle horizontally in front of RV's. "Now tell me why did you lie about the wink?" Sonam said panting for breath.

RV rested his elbows on the handle, rested his chin on his locked hands and said, "Because I wanted to see your amazing wink again and again." Sonam gave a naughty smile accompanied with an equally naughty wink. But RV winked back in an outrageously seducive manner.

15

RV lay down in his bed, chewing the cud of Sonam's wink and started feeling guilty about his anger. "Anything ugly, whatever and however small it might be, should never spoil Sonam's day," RV spoke in his mind. "I am not going to let this happen again." RV almost said it aloud and typed on his phone – 'How to control anger' and started his search on the internet.

'Take deep breaths.' RV narrowed his eyebrows as he read option one and moved on to the next which said 'Meditate'. RV kept reading next options in the hope that something interesting and doable would come up. "I think I should be able to curb it myself." RV said it aloud to himself and shut off the search engine. He slept peacefully, quite convinced that he will not let any unpleasant situation arise.

"I just can't believe it RV that we are getting to live here and even being paid in the name of summer job," Sonam forked her fingers inside her hair to shake off water after a swim. The one'o clock sun rays were at such an angle that the hillock which cupped the pool provided shade to half of the poolside. RV and Sonam enjoyed their fresh lime soda siting by the hillock's shade.

"I have decided I am going to make this kind of thing as my profession," Sonam said after a long sip of fresh lime.

"Yeah actually yes, making a life out of something that you enjoy. It will be like a dream come true," as RV said this, Sonam saw a drop of water trickle from his hair and settle on his eyelashes.

"Don't move," Sonam said and abruptly got up to scoop out the water drop with her nail. "This idea of buying a resort and making a holiday our job, we had finalized before also. Now we are going to seal the deal," saying that, she transferred the water from her finger to his thumb. She rubbed her thumb over his, quite like the thumb seal. The thumb parted after a few hard and soft rubs.

RV brought her thumb near his lips and kissed it. The hum in their bodies changed to a throb.

"RV, let's go sit on those high chairs. There is shade now." Sonam slid herself on this high stool to reach higher for fun. "I want to have a pizza for lunch here," Sonam said as she adjusted her feet on the foot rest of the stool.

"Okay. Shiv and Veer will be at the restaurant. They will have lunch there as they pick up tourists interested in our truck ride," RV said.

"I'll ask Aditi," Sonam said, dialling her number. "Aditi, want to have pizza? Join us at the pool side. Okay, see you at five thirty then."

"Aditi says she had heavy breakfast and no lunch for her." Sonam said putting down the phone.

"Nothing like a hot pizza after a swim," Sonam said taking a bite, enjoying the cheese melting in her mouth as natural curls formed by drying hair framed her face. RV's partly wet hair gave him a Greek god look. RV noticed the touch and go game played by the lips with the lipstick. RV got so involved watching that his chewing became very slow.

"What happened RV, dont you like the pizza?" Sonam asked looking up so innocently, not knowing that she was the culprit for not letting him eat.

"No, it's delicious," RV said for the taste of her lips, which trickled from the kiss during the dance near the swimming pool.

"Ya they made it well," Sonam said thinking RV was talking about the pizza. RV could not help looking at her without even blinking an eyelid.

Sonam raised both her eyebrows to ask, "What happened?" and her hands also opened up in gesture.

"I am trying to figure out if you have figured out what I had told you at the bench that day early in the morning."

"Oh! That like the grass, the sky figure out when the sun rises," Sonam said with a naughty smile dancing on her lips, making them all the more irresistable as she emptied sachets of oregano on her pizza.

"I have figured out to quite an extent." Sonam replied but RV got lost looking at her lips and hardly heard what she said. He got up to touch them, but only to remove a crust of Pizza stuck to her cupid bow. Sonam snatched the piece from his hand with her mouth, thanks to her impulsive naughty behaviour.

"I don't let go of tasty things," she said and winked.

"Your wink is getting better and better," RV said and picked up his piece of pizza, trying to calm his nerves with just a touch of her lips with his hand, but his nerves had become rebellious. "Sonam, let's start walking to our truck."

"There is still time. It's only five; we are leaving with the guests by six."

"I know, but let's go see the arrangements and receive our tourists," RV said, but in reality, her lips were causing this restlessness in him.

"OK, let's go," Sonam said as she took her hand bag and her off shoulder blue denim dress made her look ready for the long drive.

"RV, let's try getting down from the mountain side." RV's heart jumped up as he thought the way would provide for a perfect opportunity to kiss. They walked and climbed down the skirt of the mountain which had frills of grass and rocks.

Sonam stood with her back resting on the huge rock embedded like a stud on this skirt. "Come here RV, we will take a selfie." RV came and leaned on the rock next to her and she gave her phone to RV to click. She adjusted her hair and looked into the phone, trying to bring all her good mood into the selfie. "No, not good. We will have to take it again," Sonam said just when the selfie was clicked.

"Now what happened… you want to change the angle of the phone?"

"No, my lipstick! Half of it is gone. I ate it with the pizza. With my lipstick on, I feel dressed and my mood too elevates. I have forgotten to put one in my bag."

"Doesn't matter, your lips are anyway irresistible," RV said.

"I want to make them enticing." She was at her impulsive mischievousness. "Wait, wait! Let me check in my bag." She thrust her right foot against the rock to make a bar of her thigh to keep her hand bag. "I found both – lipstick and lip pencil, but no mirror," she said trying to dig her hand into various pockets of the bag. She started to open the lipstick while thinking how would she get the edges right. "I can use the selfie mode to apply. RV, please show me the phone."

"Let me try applying it for you." RV took the lipstick from her hand. She offered her lips to apply. "Let's take out the old lipstick first." RV slipped the lipstick in his pocket. He dragged his lips over hers, first left then right. As RV stroked her lips, Sonam was discovering new colours and textures of love. Yes, passion too, but passion with love is a lethal combination. The lips met each other in soft strokes, which made the rock against which Sonam rested feel like a soft cushion. He left her lips only to admire the now nude lips. They became fuller with love. RV rested his arm on the rock near her face as he now stroked her lips with his eyes, just by looking at them. Sonam's eyes were still closed. RV took out the lipstick opened it and started to apply the same on her lips. The drag of the lipstick, on her surrendered lips made her open her eyes, only to get high on his good looks. RV lined the outer lip with the lip pencil and came to stand next to her and say, "Now let's take a selfie," and he clicked.

"I am all ready for the ride RV." Sonam gave a nudge to RV with her shoulder. When they reached the truck, Shiv, Veer and Aditi were already there. Aditi and Sonam started to set the mattresses and cushions. "Aditi, help me tuck the bedsheets." Sonam and Aditi tucked the thick plain cotton sheets, giving the truck a decked up homely feel with a spirit of adventure. The reddish orange rays of the sun blowed over a few clouds as they went about their evening ride.

"Sir, ma'am, you can remove your shoes in this bag and you can make yourself comfortable inside. You can try your hand at drums, guitars and other instruments. The truck gang felt proud and happy about their creation – "Trucks and Trucks of Love." The truck now floated on the road, enjoying the mild evening breeze, just as the clouds above did.

This truck with fifteen tourists of all age groups, families, children with of-course one thing in common – young at heart – was now passing through a small village sitting in the shrubby desert with houses painted blue. RV and Sonam sat on the crown of the truck. They could see the earth running along with the sky for a long distance before embracing each other. They sat circling their knees with their arms with some space between their shoulders for the breeze to dance through. They turned to look at each other and their eyes met to toast their surreal relationship.

"RV, Sonam these kids want to sit there," Aditi called out from the body of the truck with some kids looking at Sonam and RV, all eager to come there.

"Come, we will make you all fit in somehow." Shiv picked up the younger ones to pass them to RV and he made them sit with Sonam, who circled her arm around them. The kids waved to their parents.

The embrace of the sky and earth was becoming bigger and tighter and visibility became lesser and lesser. The kids and also the people who stood looking out from the edge of the truck spotting deer, sambar, hares, could now even feel happy imagining something in the dusk far away. The truck turned its attention to fairy lights, now leaving the earth and the sky in its embrace. The tourists sang in all kinds of tunes and pitches, and played the instruments whatever little way they could, but their tune of enjoyment was just right and so the rest did not matter.

The truck reached the desert resort all lit up in diffused lights. "Wow!" The tourist felt their feet sinking in the desert. Some ran over it to see how fast they could run, some walked. "We need to come here in winters." Some tourists discussed with each other and RV and Sonam just smiled at each other, thinking of their dream.

RV and Sonam could feel the specks of sand on their lips dancing in thuds of passion and love. Sonam walked over the sand, reached the last point of the lit up sand and looked at the silhouette of the sand dunes and the village. RV had got busy talking to the tourists when Sonam had started walking and now when he looked around trying to find her, he saw her at the far end.

RV walked up to her and circled his arms around her while resting his chin on her head. "This is so beautiful," Sonam said.

"Ya, these sand dunes," RV replied looking where she was looking.

"I was talking of the way you have held me," Sonam replied.

"I am happy that you also think so," and he slid his hands to tighten the grip. They stood there for sometime, feeling secure in each other's love. RV slid his hands back and walked back to where everyone was.

Glass vases and glass lamps flickered their light over this open to sky restaurant done up in a very contemporary way. A bit of rustic touch was blown, which rooted the resort where it belonged. Mostly everybody sat on chairs placed with a long wooden table and some starters were being served hot.

"Come Sonam, I have kept tandoori aloo in your plate," Aditi called out, showing her a chair next to her. RV went and sat with Shiv, Veer and other tourists. The truck gang had organised this novel idea with so much passion that the tourists were no longer tourists. Antique transparent glass lamps with thick belly and long snout sat on this wooden table, slowly breathing light. RV and Sonam exchanged glances through this breath of light. Romance slowly breathed, giving life to love.

The truck was on its way back at around one. Some kids had slept and others enjoyed the laziness induced by the three-course meal listening to soft guitar that somebody played in the body of the truck. RV was slowly steering the truck on this empty road with Sonam sitting by his side.

"RV, I love travelling in the night," Sonam said adjusting her back against the seat.

"Why?" RV asked.

"Because I have not travelled late in the night before," Sonam replied twisting towards RV.

"I thought you would say you like this night drive because it is with me," RV replied a little dejected.

"Of course, I would not like it with just anybody. I was going to say with you, but you interrupted me with your why," Sonam said with her nothing-to-be-held-back attitude.

"You are just adorable," RV said.

RV saw two lights approaching fast towards them. RV drove slow, feeling responsible for taking so many people in the truck and also feeling love and romance all around him. RV realized that the vehicle was speeding almost head on. He became more careful. The jeep driver was in a wired mood. He kept on coming straight. Sensing this, RV became even more careful.

Sonam also realized what was happening and she yelled, "RV, careful!" By that time, the Jeep was almost head-on and RV took a sharp left cut. The jeep tried to go their left, but the high speed did not let the driver control it and the Jeep hit the tree.

RV stopped the truck, jumped out of it and went and caught hold of the driver who was a young man. The strong bumper and the bumper guard prevented any injury to the four boys who were in the open Jeep. RV caught hold of the driver and started to bash him. He rained blows on his face and stomach and the guy was already bleeding. Even though three of the boy's friends tried to pull RV away, RV managed to keep them away by hitting them too. As Sonam had seen the Jeep coming, she was also very angry at the jeep driver. She was initially very satisfied with the way RV hit them, but when she realised that RV was hitting a bit too much, she was scared. Shiv, Veer and Aditi also jumped out of the truck. Shiv and Veer caught RV and tried to pacify him. Aditi, Sonam and some guests stood near the truck, equally scared and upset.

"This bastard would have died and his friends would also have died. Just because I was slow, I was able to save them. These buggers had taken on a flight to hell. They have spoilt our trip and troubled the tourists. I am not going to leave them," and RV again came in rage, ready to hit the four guys.

"It is okay, RV. Let the police handle this," Shiv said dialling 100.

"Yes! Call the police we will tell them how much you have hit our friend," one of the guys said.

"What did you say?" RV managed to hit this guy and this time Shiv and Veer also slapped the guy who said this. "Because of people like you, lovely night rides get hijacked," RV said as his face was still red with anger.

They heard the police siren. The open Jeep guys were drunk also and by what everyone told the police, not much had to be done or explained. They made them sit in their police van and the damaged Jeep was attached to be towed.

"RV, I will drive now, you and Sonam relax at the back. In fact, try to sleep. And everyone forget all this." Shiv opened the door of the driver's seat, Veer got in from the other side. RV pressed his locked hands on the cushion, trying to soothe his mind as he sat on the mattress. As the truck continued with its pleasant journey, the soothing breeze found its way to the truck. Sonam sat with Aditi, just opposite to RV. Sonam and Aditi rested their back on the cushion, letting its softness caress their backs. Aditi's friendship and the cool breeze had together taken the job to relax Sonam. Sonam's thick eye lashes fell and rose, opening and closing her dreamy amber eyes. RV saw, how innocently Sonam was falling asleep, holding Aditi's arm, and he felt very guilty.

'I should have sucked some ugliness out of the incident instead of adding to the trauma with my anger. It was not my job to bash them up. I should have just called the police. My job should have just been scolding them and a bit of counselling. I want to protect Sonam from anything unpleasant and I am only creating tense situations.' RV was deep in conversation in his mind and came to know that they had reached only when he saw Aditi waking up Sonam.

16

"RV, why did you get so angry?" Shiv asked while driving the truck. They were taking the truck for servicing to a service station. RV didn't reply; he just looked straight out of the windscreen as he sat between Shiv and Veer. He was almost sure that his extreme anger would hamper Sonam's figuring out their relationship.

"RV, the way you were bashing the guys, you would have injured them seriously and there would have been big trouble," Veer said.

"And it's not our job. Our job was to call the police and the rest would be taken care of by them," Shiv added changing gear.

"My parents, right from my childhood days usually stay out, so I started getting angry out of irritation or for some attention seeking." This is all he could come up with after thinking the whole night. "But how my anger problem started is not of any consequence. Now I want to get rid of it. Cure myself of it," RV said feeling a little better talking about it with his friends.

"Some people say meditation is a good way to control anger," Shiv said as his eyes stayed on the road, looking through the mirage on the tar road as the hot afternoon sun played a prank with it.

"I am thinking of trying meditation," RV said.

"Meditation, are you serious RV? Meditation will be very boring." Veer turned to look at RV who continued to look straight, deep in thoughts.

"I guess all things that are used to cure something are boring like when you fall sick you go see the doctor or hospital, boring isn't it." RV said, slowly preparing himself to do some drab stuff to cure himself of his anger.

"True," Veer agreed.

"I don't want to burn her presence with my anger," RV said hammering his determination to stay calm.

"Yes, I also noticed Sonam got very scared," Shiv said.

"And your love for her tells us that her bubbly nature and sparkling face should be kept intact," Veer said.

"You guys know how I feel for her?"

RV turned to look at Veer who gave him a naughty smile and said, "We and our truck know everything, but even strangers can understand when they see you both." Shiv playfully nudged his shoulder taking advantage of the clear road.

"You guys know everything, so tell me how should I control my anger?"

Veer took a deep breath and said, "Take a deep breath and slowly exhale," and he too exhaled his breath.

"Does this really work?" RV said as he practiced a few exhales and inhales.

"It should. I saw one guru telling on the channel this technique of controlling anger while I was surfing channels," Veer replied.

"See what google has to say," Shiv suggested.

"Ya, I had checked, some stupid things came up... count till ten, practice self talking, etc.," RV said.

"If you start self-talking a bit loud, Sonam will think you have gone mad," Shiv said as he laughed.

"And if she starts thinking I am mad, she will never say 'I love you'."

"Whether she thinks or doesn't, you are mad, mad about Sonam," Veer said and Shiv banged the horn 2-3 times to second Veer and the three friends laughed enjoying this light moment.

They had reached the service station and Shiv parked the truck. The place was big with petrol bunks; many mechanics were busy checking the tyres and putting oil. The three friends walked into a shop at the petrol station with all kinds of eatables and books. When they picked up a chilled can of Sprite and held in their hand, the heat of the day melted in the chill of the moment.

"Meditation camp from six in the morning till nine in the night," Shiv read written on a phamplet stuck to the wall opposite to them where they stood in the shop.

RV gluped the sip to ask, "Where are you reading this?" and before Shiv pointed to the wall, both RV and Veer realized that it was written on the pamphlet.

"That is why it is said if you have decided to do something, you will find the means," Veer commented.

"This meditation camp is also somewhere near our resort," RV said finishing his Sprite.

"Yes, you go for one day and see if you like it, and of course, we can manage things for one day at the resort," Veer said.

"Shiv, buy some chocolates for Sonam and Aditi and we will go find the mechanic to get our truck checked." RV and Veer put the tins in the bins and went out.

With a few more instructions to the mechanic and they themselves hovering over the bonnet, their truck was ready in about two hours.

Their truck started even more smoothly after this extra pampering at the service centre.

"Aditi and Sonam must have started today's holiday flavour at the resort. We are back just in time," RV said.

Aditi and Sonam's faces brightened up on seeing them and their hearts melted after they got the chocolates. Some of the kids jumped up on seeing RV, Veer and Shiv as they knew them and some new kids who didn't know them still jumped looking at the other kids jump. The chocolates were enough for the kids too.

"Didi, this is molten," a cute four-year-old kid said as he tried to open the wrapper, with his mouth watering.

"Yes, we eat it like chocolate sauce," Sonam said. She opened the wrapper and exposed the chocolate after uncovering its shiny golden silver wrapping. She dipped her tongue and lips into this smooth sweet brown pleasure. Then she looked up with her eyes still closed in pleasure and she licked the chocolate on her lips and beyond. Everyone there including Veer, Aditi and Shiv imitated her to eat their chocolate.

"I love chocolates," RV said aloud, but 'more on your lips' in his mind and he too started eating it.

One small boy rubbed his hands together, spreading the smooth chocolate over them and said, "My hands look so nice."

Another boy made Rambo lines on his face with his chocolaty fingers and said, "You look like Rambo 8."

"Make these Rambo lines for me also," another kid asked the boy next to her. The kids got busy with smearing each other's face with chocolate lines with some using their chocolate from the wrapper too.

"Didi, show me your cheek," a boy told Sonam and the kids were so pleased with themselves by giving Rambo lines to RV, Aditi, Sonam, Veer and Shiv too.

"Now all of us are a Rambo army, but where is our ammunition?" Sonam announced. Everyone looked at her with surprise.

"But we didn't get our toy guns here," some kids said.

"Forget guns, I have grenades for you." Sonam dropped a bomb with her breaking news.

"Grenades?" everyone sighed. RV, Shiv, Veer and Aditi too looked puzzled.

"I have many colours of smoke grenades," Sonam said.

"Sonam, this is a killing idea. But when did you buy this?" Veer and Aditi asked.

"From Jaipur, I don't miss such fun things," Sonam said. Let's all walk down to my room to get the smoke grenades.

"Didi, I want red," one small boy held Sonam's hand as he walked on the down slope road.

"I want blue," another small boy said as he held Sonam's other hand. The other kids held hands of the others. The kids entertained the truck band with various stories about school as they walked.

"Guys, I will get our grenades in two minutes," and Sonam went to her room.

"Be careful everyone. I am opening the pin of the grenade. 5, 4, 3, 2, 1," Sonam said as she opened one and boom! Red smoke rose and spread in all patterns. All kids got one grenade. Some sat on the big rock in front of the rooms while others stood on the road. Everyone opened the pin and out came orange, blue green, light blue smoke, making them feel like Rambo. Some ran on the road just to enjoy the trail of smoke, some just sat seeing their smoke make different patterns of smoke in the air. The whole place was bombarded with enjoyment. Can anyone think of giving real granades to kids or throwing grenades at them? Hello there, is the world listening?

The early evening sun rays courted RV's hazel eyes and ruffled hair, lighting up his face by their affair. RV's shoes were embeded in the grass which was going wild over the sun rays as they were also trying to woo RV. The grass grew wild with rage over a vast level area restricting the trees only to a few. Various colours and shapes of young wild flowers tried to rise above the grass to woo RV. No matter how much anybody tried, there was only one strong affair of RV and Sonam, which was on its way to become a love story.

RV watched Sonam collect wild flowers along with other tourist they had got along. Shiv and Veer were helping the tourists set the easel in this huge open area. Aditi was distributing colours. Anyone who wished to paint this beautiful landscape could paint; feel the joy of creation in its own little way. The other family members of the person who painted were collecting wild flowers, grass and twigs to paste to the painting to give the painting a unique 3-D effect. Sonam was busy helping the tourists pluck various things to adorn the painting. Sonam scooped out a cluster of tiny purple flowers which grew almost touching the ground.

"This is mind blowing. I also want to stick it to a painting." Holding their delicate stems in her hand, she looked up to call RV. "RV, that day I painted at the hilltop restaurant; today it is your turn. I want to add these wild flowers to the painting."

"Okay," RV called out. RV set his canvas on his easel and with a colour palette on its side, he looked up, holding a brush and saw Sonam. "Sonam, don't move… just stay there, I am painting you," RV called out.

"Yeah!" Sonam jumped up.

"I have told you to stay still."

"Ok," Sonam said as she slightly slanted her head up and the sun rays spread over her irrestible face. Sonam in her bluish green dress almost looked part of the landscape. RV wanted to run, go lift her and kiss her, but instead picked the brush to paint.

White speck-like flowers of reed grass brushed the tip of her fingers. The grass only reached her ankles while a few flowers of the grass could sway with the edge of her dress, touching her knees. The breeze was mild and just enough for the flimsy material of her dress and the wild flowers to tango. RV used all shades of sky blue to create a back drop of the sky and brushed orange and red too to dress the sky for the evening. RV drew Sonam's outline and the dress around her. RV was not a trained painter, but if a person has a passion, no training is required.

Sonam was still, but her gaze was not. Her gaze saw some butterflies. Sonam started running to be part of this gang of naughty butterflies. RV watched Sonam run with her hair flying back and her dress fluttered. RV saw his painting and the sunlight fast turning to orange, so he called for Sonam.

"Sonam come back to your position. If I don't finish the painting, where will you put the flowers?"

"Coming," Sonam said and she was back. RV tried everything to get texture and life into the painting. He tried making the fall of her dress look natural, using his fingers, making the paint thick and thin at places. He used different types of brushes and strokes. He ran his eyes over his finished painting looking a little longer at Sonam in the painting and wondered, how could he ever get her beauty on the canvas.

"I don't believe this!" Sonam stood next to him admiring the painting. Sonam started to stick the flowers she had collected on the canvas, on her plain dress. As RV guided her hand to write RS at right corner of the canvas, Sonam felt RS being engraved on her heart. Seeing RV and Sonam, the sun also decided to go look for romance and called it a day.

The tourists, RV and others picked up the easels, paints and the painting, to walk back to the resort. The paintings, whether done perfectly or not, complete or not complete, it was a precious souvenir for everybody. Enjoyment should not be lost on the way to perfection.

Shiv stopped to announce, "Anyone who wants to complete the painting can also do it tomorrow evening."

"Yes, that will be great, RV. Tomorrow I will paint you," Sonam said as she adjusted her painted canvas in the other hand.

"No Sonam, tomorrow I am going for a meditation camp for the whole day," RV replied. Sonam suddenly felt the whole energy and romance drawn out of her body. She could not ask how or why. Images of boring meditation camps where she used to accompany her parents flashed across her mind. "No TV and music today, my kirtan friends are coming to do kirtan at the house," her mom's voice bombared in her head. "Put off the TV; come for the evening pooja," her father's voice too travelled in her head. She could feel the brass pooja bells in her hand whether she wanted to play them or not. She was only a child and when she wanted her parents to do some childlike fun stuff with her, they did just the opposite.

They thought god will bless her if she did all that, but they forgot god would first want their creations to be happy. Her parents never realized that and as they found their happiness in ashrams, with too many poojas, strict regime to sleep on time, getting up early for meditation, they expected their daughter to find her happiness their way.

Sonam's way of loving and thanking god was different. She always wanted to have fun with lots of madness, music and dance. She believed, what better way to worship and thank god than to enjoy the life which god had created. Sonam loved to dress, her other way to worship god. She wanted to take interest in what she wore, how she wore, to take care and celebrate god's creation – herself. She wanted to be happy and spread happiness.

She was walking with RV back to the resort, but was in her own thoughts and was not listening to anything that RV told her about the meditation camp.

"Sonam, do you want to come there? The others can manage here."

"No RV, I want to stay here and paint tomorrow. I don't want to do this," was the only polite answer she could think of.

17

Sonam could hear some baba giving gyan and gyan on TV in his typical style. Sonam hated it, and to block the sound, she rolled to her side on the bed and covered her ear with the pillow. But the voice of the baba was stubborn and entered her sandwitched head. She threw the pillow away and sat up cross-legged, looking at the blank TV

"Oh! I am still at the resort room. And the TV is off. Thank god for that." She came out of her room in the open. She walked over the road feeling the freshness. She tried to walk fast, trying to push the thought that RV was at some meditation camp.

The sun shone hotter than usual at this morning time and sprinkled beads of sweat over her face. She felt hot and humid and went back to her room. Walk had not done her any good and she felt miserable. All her excitement had come to an end and she buried her head in the pillow and forced herself to sleep. Sound of vigrously played chimtas bombarded in her head. She sat up abruptly and pressed her ears with her palm. As her eyes skimmed the room, she realized it was her phone ringing.

She was relieved to pick it up to say "Hello!"

"The breakfast is about to close. It is eleven. Come fast, we are all here." This was Shiv on the line.

"Shiv, I am not hungry and very tired. I will come directly for lunch."

"OK, you rest; we will tell you what we discussed at lunch."

"Ya," Sonam answered and again slipped back to sleep. Whenever Sonam felt depressed, she used to sleep, but would wake up feeling all the more miserable. She loved life, all fun, and if she overslept, she would feel she had wasted a few precious hours of life sleeping.

Her dreams were reminding her of all the things she wanted to forget.

She woke up at two with a heavy head.

'I think I am over-reacting. Going for a meditation camp does not make RV boring. These days, meditation has become a fad. Actually there is nothing wrong also. It is only me who finds it boring.' With this little pep talk, Sonam got up and started to dress to go for lunch at the restaurant of the resort. Sonam climbed down the steps wearing a nice dress and a coat of dark red lipstick to paint her mood cheerful. She thud her feet playfully on the last few steps, living up to the promise of staying happy to herself. A very uncomfortable restlessness had creaped in her body which she was trying to ignore.

"Hi everybody," Sonam added that extra cheerfulness in her voice as she greeted everybody sitting on their favourite table so that some of the cheerfulness got reflected back to her. "How come our most energetic Sonam got tired today?" Veer asked.

"Sonam has been so active all these days. So, one day getting up late, you can grant her that," Aditi said.

"Not when we are here and RV is not there," Veer said with a naughty smile.

"Veer, you have a point there. Sonam, maybe we are not as special as RV, but we are great friends now," Aditi was at her playful way.

"Stop teasing Sonam," Shiv put his arm around Sonam with affection.

"OK, I will never oversleep in the room."

"Great, as a tribute to this sweet promise, let's start our lunch with dessert first," Shiv led her to a chair next to him.

"Done." Sonam gave a thumbs up. They sat on the table next to a huge glass which gave them a feel of being next to the hillocks and trees while enjoying the chill of the air conditioner inside.

"We are all missing RV," Shiv said digging his spoon in a smooth brownie.

"We definitely feel incomplete," Aditi said eating her ice-cream.

"We and our truck will fetch him at night," Veer said.

Sonam's vanilla ice-cream melted in her mouth and the smoothness evened out her restlessness. Was it the ice-cream or the fact that she would go get RV back?

"Sonam, do you know RV is a very good football player? And football became very popular in our school because of him." Veer said as he sat after getting his plate filled with rotis and some curries.

"Really?" Sonam asked as she got up to go with Shiv to get food.

"But not because he played well, but because all the girls came to see football because of him," Shiv said.

"RV's passion was only sport and not girls. He would not even look at them," Aditi added.

"Poor girls would be dying for his attention," Veer said sitting opposite to Shiv.

"We were so surprised when he told us about you Sonam and the trip he planned for you with all his attention on you," Veer said.

"And we are all so greatful for his grand idea of the trip because of which we are having so much fun," Veer and Aditi said almost together and Shiv showing his thumbs up as he chewed his food.

Sonam was so flattered and more in love with herself. 'RV is a great guy. I should not get any stupid throughts about meditation go in my head,' Sonam said in her mind as she went around choosing things from the buffet.

After lunch, as it was a hot afternoon, they took the golf cart till the club house. There were good two hours for their fun dance with the kids when they reached the club house. They sat on the peacock blue floor cushions.

"We cannot let go of our truck gang," Shiv spoke with a tone which said he meant what he was saying.

"Who says we are letting it go," Aditi said casually.

"This summer job will be over soon and I feel like making this our permanent job," Shiv continued.

"Yes, me and RV also want to buy the truck, make our own resort," Sonam said.

"This is the idea of the century," Veer said keeping his phone away.

"Guys, reality check, a lot of money is required for this. From where will we get that?" Aditi put forth her genuine doubts.

"Let's dream big first. The dreams will make way," Shiv replied.

"True, first we dream big and then put all our energy to make it a reality," Aditi also agreed.

"How about making a big barn here for our music shows?" Veer pulled himself deep into the conversation.

"A barn!" rest of them said it together.

"Let's chalk out the barn of our dreams. Veer, get a chart-paper and a pencil, we will draw the design right away," Sonam told Veer.

"Ya, I am sure these club house people must be having it," Veer said as he got up to get the stuff.

Shiv, Aditi and Sonam sat quietly, weaving their common dream.

"Come guys, there is a drawing table in this coffee shop here." Veer took them all with him. He kept the pencil in the middle of the sheet and drew two slanting lines for the roof of the barn. He made a perfect slanting slope in one go. When the heart is into something, things always fall in place.

"Give me the pencil, Veer," Shiv took the pencil from Veer and drew a horizontal line joining the slope while making it stand on two vertical lines from its edge for the side wall.

"We make this with big rafters for our band to perform," Shiv and Veer said together.

Now Aditi took the pencil to draw. "These are the rafters for the sides which make the wooden floor at a height for the people to dance and have fun."

"We will fix ball lights and other LEDs here, hanging from the rafters," Sonam said as she took the pencil to draw circles over the line for the lights.

"Down here on the floor, we will keep some tables with nice lamps. When the lights fall on this wooden flooring, it will look so inviting for dance," Aditi said as she drew after Sonam.

"For lovely Indian weather, we will make huge windows which will stay open all the time except for very cold nights, making our truck and the fields rock together," Veer said.

"And our truck will stand here next to the barn," Shiv took the pencil to draw as he said.

Sonam now took the pencil to write, 'Trucks and trucks of love' and said, "This will glow, written in fairy lights." They all looked at each other and gave out a scream of joy before hugging each other. The kids who had come for the dance class saw them, also started giggling and hugging each other. Happiness is always infectious.

"Everybody tell me, which song do you want for dance," Aditi said to start this fun after noon.

"Where is RV bhaiya?" a cute little girl asked Sonam.

"Hi!" before Sonam could think of what to say, Aditi replied.

"RV bhaiya has gone to improve himself by learning meditation."

"But RV bhaiya is great, he need not improve," the little girl continued.

"RV has admirers everywhere," Shiv said as he and Veer came with their rolled plan on the chart paper.

Sonam was lost in her own thought thinking, "How can meditation ever be called improvement? It can only make him boring."

"Don't worry, he will come tomorrow. And for today, you can dance with us," Aditi told the little girl before putting the music and starting their fun dance.

"Trucks and Trucks of love" is what glowed in her mind as she imagined their truck next to the barn when she sat at the table under the tree sipping coffee. She looked at the white rose bud reflecting the reddish light of the evening sun. The paint fun had been postponed.

The ability to choose is a big thing in life. The truck band had taken a first step, to dream, to choose.

'I think mom and dad will give me some money to invest in this dream. Next week, when this summer job gets over, I will take RV to introduce him to my parents.' She continued her mental dialogue, '… as someone I want to spend the rest of my life with' and she smiled as she completed her mental dialogue. 'But first I have to ask RV. I will ask soon and I am sure he loves me.'

While Sonam spoke to her mind, Aditi came and hugged her from behind and said, "I am so excited about our plan of barn and truck band and I have already spoken to my parents about it and they are ready to help me with some money.

"That's great news Aditi. I am sure my parents will also help us," Sonam shared her excitement.

"We will go meet some bank managers after this summer job." Shiv and Veer were totally engrossed in this discussion as they came and sat next to Sonam and Aditi.

"Come, come let's all go to get RV. We will drive leisurely and discuss our plan on the way. Can't wait to tell RV," Shiv got up. Veer sat behind the wheel to drive, while Shiv, Aditi and Sonam squeezed next to him.

"This is the way to the pond we had gone the other day," Sonam said as she recognized the way.

"Yes, this is the same way, but we have left the turn that takes us right to the pond. As we go around this hillock, we will be able to see the pond down." Shiv told Sonam.

She looked to her left and saw the lake deep down and said, "Wow!" and everyone else also admired along with her.

"I want our farm, barn somewhere near this lake," Sonam said as she was already with the guitar at their future barn near the lake.

"This would be a perfect place," Aditi, Shiv and Veer said together.

"We can talk to some farmers around and I am sure someone will be willing to sell some land," Shiv said.

"Yes and to start with, we take a small piece of land and as we start making profit, we will keep increasing our area," Aditi suggested.

RV was coming out of the meditation camp and was not very happy about his day. 'Why did I come here? The summer job is getting over soon. I have wasted a precious day without Sonam. My anger is not a big problem right now, but it might increase. I was drunk the first time Sonam saw me as I was frustrated over mom dad asking me to join business. Sonam did not mind that, but I won't spoil things ever.'

As RV was in deep conversation with himself, he realized he was out of the gate of the camp. He tried to look for a bus to go back to the resort. The boring hostage day just freed him when he saw his friends.

"RV, we missed you so much." All of them hugged him.

"I have just been away a few hours," RV said with a smile.

"We have an exciting plan which we wanted to share as soon as possible," Shiv said.

"We are going to make a living with our truck gang," Aditi poured her excitement in this sentence. RV looked at Sonam with an expression that came only with love, excitement and dreams. RV circled his arms around Shiv and Aditi and said looking at Veer and Sonam standing opposite to him. "Sonam and I had dreamt this kind of thing, but now I feel we can make it a reality too, with you all."

"RV, we have a plan of our barn where we will have our music and fun," Sonam told him.

"Yes RV, here is the plan we all drew," Shiv said.

"You also add what you want," Veer suggested.

"Here, let's show him with the truck lights." Aditi took the chart near the head lights.

"This won't be very comfortable. We'll stop at some dhabha on the way." Veer suggested and they all jumped at the back of the truck, while Shiv drove.

"How was the meditation camp?" Aditi asked.

"Quite fruitful, they were saying there are many advantages of meditation," RV said, justifying his going for the camp to himself.

Sonam gave a light nudge to RV's shoulder and said, "Did you miss me?" as both of them stood on the box looking outside, enjoying the breeze.

"Why should I miss you?" RV teased her.

"Becuase, I am a very cute girl who is so much fun to be with," as Sonam turned towards the crown of the truck and spreads her arms feeling her hair being pushed back by the wind.

This made RV fall for Sonam all over again and he told himself he will pursue his meditation to curb his anger.

"Here is the dhabha with good lights," Sonam said as she spotted a few lights.

"Shiv, stop at this dhabha," Sonam called out banging her hand on the body of the truck. The others also joined in this banging to increase the effect and of course to drum out fun. Shiv too responded by banging the outside of the door as he stopped at the dhaba.

Shiv spread the chart paper on a table. Veer kept four glasses at four corners to hold the chart. Everyone started to explain to RV what they had drawn as their heads almost touched bending over the chart.

"RV, we will start searching for a piece of land available near the pond," Sonam said. RV could imagine himself with Sonam on this farm, making life with wonderful friends. He almost felt strings of the guitar on his fingers, the barn coming alive with their music and the people who were high on life.

RV didn't want his dream world to ever get blotted with his anger, and at the moment, the only saviour of his anger was meditation so he said, "People who come to stay with us can be given an option of meditation by the pond."

"Yes, a good idea, and our foreign clients will especially love it," Shiv added.

Sonam felt a string of the guitar break as she had kept her fingers on it, imagining herself on the raft, playing it.

'How can RV forget we had thought of taking tourists for a splash and wash our truck?' Sonam thought as she looked at the bulb which formed a part of the canopy of wires, with bulbs trying to dry her watery eyes.

For the first time, she went against her impulsive behaviour and did not say what she felt. She didn't want RV to change his idea because she disapproved it so strongly. And it wasn't just about changing the idea. She wanted to know what really made up RV. She had known RV for around a month now and she thought she knew everything about him. She was so close to figuring out, in fact, she was just there.

'May be people can hide their real self for a while and their true self seeps out sooner or later.' Sonam was deep in thoughts. Sonam didn't want to colour RV's thoughts as these would fade with time. Sonam wanted to see what colours RV was made of. All these days, Sonam was quite sure she knew RV. But what was this new colour which she had missed seeing. This was the colour which she detested all her life. There is nothing bad or good about a colour. It is just that some people like a particular colour, while others don't.

"Bhaiya, we are soon going to open a unique resort. We will get our tourists to your dhaba for food." Sonam was pulled out of her mental dialogue when Aditi told this to the person who got food for them.

"They will like our food a lot, ma'am," the person said, feeling important.

Sonam had totally missed what all discussion went on among her friends as she was in deep thoughts.

"Sonam eat, you haven't even started," RV said putting some curry and roti for her. Sonam looked at RV and thought although she was pushed back in saying "I love you", she knew her heart was beating for him. Maybe she was reading too much in RV's interest for meditation, which according to her made a person boring. She always thought there were better ways to stay calm or unwind, whatever than to meditate.

They had hot gulab jamuns after dinner to celebrate their grand plan.

18

They had found one acre of land amist fields quite near the lake after two days of talking to locals near the pond. The land was only worth five lakhs.

"My rough estimate, to begin with, we need thirty-five lakhs. We need five for the land, ten to make a simple barn, ten for the musical instruments, five for some other basic construction and one for marketing our farm cum music barn. And most importantly, we need four lakhs for our truck," Shiv said with his pencil still in his hand, sitting on the chair with his feet on the bed.

All five of them sat in similar fashion, which could be called a round-bed conference. Decision becomes great only if the people involved take the decision from their heart, have trust in their decision and have the ability to transform it into action.

"Each of us will have to arrange for seven lakhs," Aditi said.

"And as and when we start making profits, we will keep buying land around and keep expanding," Veer said.

"We will buy a few tents for the people to stay in," Sonam said.

"Soon a word will spread about our fabulous venture – 'Trucks and trucks of Love'," RV said feeling great about announcing the name of their dream venture.

"It all started with our truck trip, so the name has to be TRUCKS AND TRUCKS OF LOVE," Aditi said.

"Shiv, this is your room, so make coffee for us," RV said.

"Taking a loan from the bank will be difficult, and on top of that, high interest rates too. So I guess we can always take loan from our parents. I think if the bank does not support, our parents will support our dreams," Veer said taking a cup of hot coffee from Shiv.

"I went to Harvard on my parents' insistence, but I want to do something in India. This resort is just the thing I would love to do and make our novel concept famous world over. I want to tell the world that Indians know the best – how to have a great holiday,"RV spoke up in pride.

"What about your MBA result, Sonam?" Aditi said.

"Yes, I am sure of getting admission somewhere. I will give you this money and will come help you in holidays and will join after the course," Sonam said.

"Great!" Shiv said.

"I will call now," RV dialled. "Hi Dad. No, I told you I will not be able to come for the exhibition." RV told his dad and heard patiently before he replied. "But dad it's a commitment and I love this summer job. In fact, there is something very exciting I want to tell you. Dad, I and my friends want to make our own farm house kind of resort. I want you to help me with about seven lakhs..." RV got up and went out of the room while he was talking.

"Sonam, we will keep easels and make our tourists paint."

"We will make every day innovatively enjoyable for them," Sonam replied to Aditi.

Shiv and Veer also brought their energy and innovative ideas into the discussion of their dream.

Sonam looked at RV when he entered the room and her smile vanished when she saw his face red with anger. "Hey, it's okay RV, we will be able to convince your parents with time," Shiv said as he also understood something was wrong when he saw RV come in the room.

"Damn my parents," RV said and with a closed fist he hit the lamp shade which innocently glowed on the side table. RV had hit straight, but things never fall straight in anger. The lamp deviated to the left and hit Sonam's leg before falling down. The glass of the bulb broke into pieces, scattering over and around her feet. Sonam was too shocked to dust off the glass pieces fallen over her feet.

Sonam was stunned, not because RV broke the lamp, but because she felt for him... thinking what was it that his parents had said on the phone that he became so violent. RV's eyes now bled seeing glass pieces lay over Sonam's delicate soft feet. He just looked and felt the prick in his eyes while Shiv and Veer picked up the pieces. Although Sonam was unscratched, RV was not. RV was badly bruised because of what had happened because of his anger; he left and went to his room.

Sonam also felt uneasy and started to follow him to his room. RV was very angry at himself now. As it was his fist which broke the glass, he entered his room and banged his fist against the mirror. He felt some pain which his eyes had felt looking at pieces on Sonam's feet eaze out.

"RV, what have you done?" Sonam screamed when she saw all this. "It's okay if your parents didn't agree, they will understand if you try telling them differently and patiently," Sonam said pulling glass pieces out of his blood-stained hand.

RV could not say anything. He just pressed his teeth together. "Come here now!" Sonam pulled him near the wash basin and started washing his hand, lightly rubbing with her hand. He gulped, overwhelmed by her affection and his behaviour.

Sonam picked up one of his bandanas to tie the hand and said, "Come, let's go to our favourite bench and we will figure out what can be done." She circled her arm around his waist and his arm automatically went over her shoulders as they started walking with the wind caressing him.

"Every problem has a solution if tackled with a cool mind. Now tell me, what did your parents say?" Sonam asked as they settled on the bench looking at the mountains, and this time the sun was on its way to go behind them. The grass around, the bench had grown taller than last time, as if eager to hear what RV had to say.

"My parents are dead against the idea of the resort. They want me to join and participate in their diamond business. They are thinking I will be wasting my harward MBA degree," RV was able to say this effordlessly.

"It is okay, RV. Parents also dream for us and sometimes our dreams clash with theirs. We should give them some time to understand our dreams and if we have a real passion for our dreams, sooner or later, they will understand."

Sonam's innocent way of explaining put a smile back on RV's lips and the determination to weed away anger back firm in his mind.

"Look at me," RV said and opened her left eye then right with his thumb and index finger.

"Now what are you checking?" Sonam asked unable to understand.

"I am trying to see where so much of wisdom hidden under your naughty eyes is?" And then he hugged her and both felt complete. The wild grass around them made waves triggered by the wind and the hug.

RV did not think meditation was boring. He wanted to follow everything religiously whatever the meditation camp people had told him. He was determined to get rid of his anger. RV got up from his bed, stretched his body as the sun also woke up. RV looked out of his window and saw plants growing lazily in the mud. 'I have rosary beads in my jeans.' The brown colour of the mud reminded him of them.

He sat on the bench just next to his room and started turning the rosary beads with his thumb on his index finger. RV looked at the sky, while RV's mind only thought of Sonam. True love is also meditation. It gives peace of mind and feels good but this did not occur to RV.

Sonam had also gotten up early and felt a certain beckoning by the bench where RV and she usually sat. Sonam quickened her steps so that she could be there for as much time as possible before the sunrise. She sat there alone, waiting for RV, with the wild grass and flowers too joining her in the wait.

She got restless after waiting for an hour and decided to go get him from his room. Sonam saw him with the rosary beads and the sight was repulsive for her. She remembered that her father and mother often sat turning beads, which made the atmosphere of the house very dull. As a child, she had pulled apart many rosaries and had got scolded because of it. Sonam's impulsive nature urged her to snatch the rosary from RV's hand and rip it apart, but something stopped her. What if he just stopped this meditation business to make her feel good? But his liking – or that's what Sonam thought at the moment – would not change permanently. She could not take that risk with her life.

Sonam turned and went back to her room as tears rolled down her check. 'Lively beautiful happening life is not in my fate,' Sonam spoke to herself while crying on her bed. 'RV was like a dream come true, then what happened to him suddenly? I want people to laugh, sing, dance. How can RV do such a boring thing, sitting there like a fool and I like a bigger fool waited for him.' Sonam kept thinking only negative things.

RV saw the colour of the sun brighter and he realized it was late. He ran for the bench on the fifth level where he knew Sonam waited for him. From far he could see the bench empty, and he came down to her room.

"Sonam, Sonam!" RV called out, tried her phone." Sonam was crying, so she didn't want to open the door for him. RV went back to his room, thinking Sonam was asleep.

Sonam was getting pulled in a cave of her growing up years where the day began with elaborate morning aarti and another aarti at the end of the day. Their holidays were spent at some ashram where the gurus would make her holidays unbearable with maun vrats, meditation and bland food... everything done in the name of detoxification and a cool mind. Mind becomes cool and joyful only with the things that a person enjoys and that is different for different people. Festivals for Sonam would mean visiting temples only and not much festivity at home, and she hated it. Sonam saw god in the sunrise, rain, everything in nature, music and she liked visiting a temple more if it was amist fields or a quiet hill.

When Sonam did not pick up the phone for a long time and she did not come for breakfast, RV was sure Sonam had started hating him because of his bouts of anger and its growing severity. RV panicked and thought of trying all things told at the meditation camp. There was every chance for him to loose temper as he still had to convince his parents about their venture 'Trucks and Trucks of Love'.

"What has happened? Sonam has still not come." Shiv said as he pulled his chair to sit across RV.

"Shiv, she has sent a message that she does not want to eat. But I think she is upset seeing my bouts of anger," RV replied.

"She should be," Aditi and Veer said together as they too joined them.

"I am going to try everything to control my anger," RV said and opened the Amazon app on his phone and typed: 'Aids to control anger'. He put a meditation head band, meditation candle in the cart and ordered on speed delivery of one day.

"Hello sir, okay," Shiv spoke to someone on the phone. "We will, sir," Shiv kept the phone down and said. "Some all girls' tour is arriving today. The manager says that Aditi and Sonam should plan something for this girls' trip."

"And yes take them for a cycle trip to nearby places."

"Okay," Aditi said as she got up to go to Sonam's room to plan.

"Sonam, Sonam !" Aditi called out at Sonam's room.

"Hi Aditi!" Sonam opened the door after washing her eyes.

"What happened... your eyes are swollen?" Aditi said.

"Nothing, I got some allergy." Sonam said going against her impulsive nature as she feared Aditi might tell RV. Sonam took some medicine in front of Aditi so she was convinced nothing was wrong and they started planning some fun for the ladies' trip.

The girls' trip first kept Sonam busy, but her mind only churned negative thoughts about RV, which only convinced her that if she decided to spend her life with RV, after the initial few years, he would also become boring like her parents.

'I have known RV for a month now. The time with him was like a dream come true. Maybe he was doing all kinds of fun stuff to impress me. But his inclination is for boring meditation camps.' Sonam lay in her bed, unable to sleep.

RV's Amazon courier had arrived and he was practicing meditation with the head band, trying different options available. Sonam would go to their favourite bench, sit there, see the sunrise through tears in her eyes. RV would usually over sleep, practising different options on his meditation head band. A web of misunderstandings was being woven by both RV and Sonam.

Sonam was sitting on the bench when RV came. Sonam was happy to see him there after three days and she sucked her tears.

"Sonam, I got this meditation head band. Want to try? This has an option of rain falling, birds chirping."

"No, I can directly feel nature, rain, listen right now to the chirping birds. Technology should not be intruding here," Sonam said.

"You are right," RV kept the head band away and said, "Why use it when nature is there in front of you!"

'Why use such things at all,' Sonam said in her mind. Looking at nature was her connection with god and self. It gave her joy.' Joy was the aim of all meditation techniques and gurus. Doing whatever gives a person joy is their meditation.' Sonam wanted to say it aloud, but she just said it in her mind.

Communication had stopped flowing between them. This time, no waves were created in the grass; it just stood still.

RV could see that Sonam was not the same and he thought his anger had stolen her smile and chirpiness. This made him get serious about ways to control his anger. But those ways were what irritated Sonam. It's a whole industry which is selling peace. But peace cannot be bought. Real peace and happiness can only be got with good relations.

'I will tell Sonam that I love her and will be able to curb my anger. But what if she says she would not risk staying with a person with violent tendencies for the rest of her life.' RV thought this many times in a day, but shelved the idea.

Aditi and Sonam were coming on cycles with the all girls group.

"Let's go see that fort on top of the hill," one of the tourists suggested.

"Aditi, I will wait here. I will eat sugarcanes from these fields till you all come."

"Okay," Aditi said. The light green coloured leaves of the sugarcane looked like an elegant strole that the sugarcane held. She broke one and pealed with her teeth. She stopped eating as she remembered the time she had eaten sugarcane with RV. The juice that tasted so sweet the other day tasted bland today. She stopped sucking the juice and just held on to the half-peeled sugarcane, looked deep into the sugarcane field thinking deeper and deeper.

On the way back, Aditi told Sonam that RV had tried asking his parents about the money, and they hadn't agreed. Sonam felt a little knot in her heart thinking how RV would be feeling. Sonam's heart was soaked with the lovely time she had with RV over a month now. And she was going to make a living with an idea which was given birth by her vacation which started with the solo trip. She remembered everything from the first time she saw him and what all happened after that as she pedalled her way back with the girls, oblivious of what others were conversing about.

'RV, at the meditation camp, meditation head bands, can't imagine him like that,' and she applied a strong brake to her cycle as she had reached the resort. 'RV was so pefect for me. It was too good to be true. Maybe that is why I was scared to tell him that I love him. I was scared that things would just fizzle out. My fears have come true.' Sonam was conversing with herself as she climbed the steps cut out of rocks. She was on the way to her room and RV's room came before her's.

When she stood in front of RV's room, she forgot everything that was troubling her and she wanted to run and give RV a tight hug. She almost ran, but her feet froze when she heard some mantras being played on his phone while RV was concentrating on the frame of a candle kept on the table. RV didn't realize Sonam was seeing him from the window. She retracted her steps, devastrated. 'I am going to go away, very far. I will give my share of seven lakhs and join MBA wherever I get admission. I will tell everybody that I will join after doing MBA, but won't. I can't see this boring aspect of RV. I want to remember RV for the music, dance, fun and the time we spent here.' She lay down in the hammock looking up at a clear sky, but through clouds of tears in her eyes. She could not go to her room. She needed an open space to breathe.

The sky was clear, full of stars, but there was no clarity in her eyes. Past experiences shape our perception, which create serious misunderstandings. Relations fall prey to misunderstandings. Sonam's hammock swayed a little. As there was no breeze, confused she looked to her right.

RV stood there smiling. "You didn't come to my room after coming back."

"I wanted to be here in the open," Sonam replied, giving an artificial smile.

'You could have taken me along,' RV wanted to say, but could not gather courage to say as he was sure Sonam was avoiding him because of his destructive anger.

RV also lay down next to Sonam in the hammock. Sonam rested her head on his arm and her nerves started to soothe.

"Today, there is no chance of rain," Sonam said. Her eyes dried because she felt good as RV had come looking for her.

"Sonam, look at the star there, the brightest one."

"That one?" Sonam said pointing.

"Yes, now keep looking at it, slowly inhaling and exhaling. The effect is so calming. I tried doing this with the flame of a candle in the room. It feels calming and a star also being a luminous object will be even better," RV said trying to tell Sonam that he was learning to be calm.

This time, black clouds hit her eyes like a bad storm. Sonam just wanted today's night also to be like the night they had spent in the hammock. She hated to hear 'luminous object' for a romantic star. The light of the romantic star was slowly fading in her eyes. Sonam started crying.

RV felt devastrated. RV could feel her tears on his arm and he too cried as he thought, 'I can never forgive myself for making my angel cry. I only deserve her hatred. The glass fell on her foot which looked like the worst sin. It could have been her face. Oh my god! I should stay away from her.' RV indulged in a serious mental dialogue.

"I am really sorry RV," Sonam said sobbing as she got up to go. 'RV is not at fault. Meditation has become a fad; he too has taken refuge for whatever reason it might be, but my aversion is too strong to take our relationship forward.' Sonam's conversation went on in her mind as she shut the room door behind her.

RV clasped his hands tight. He had not gathered the courage to say 'sorry' also. Being here in the hammock without Sonam was a punishment.

Harsh rays of the sun late into the morning woke him up as contrast to the sweet tickling by Sonam. RV walked back to his room, heartbroken, and he could only blame himself for his pain.

'RV planned this trip – our Trucks and trucks of love trip. I should not have made him feel so bad by crying. But I just can't wear a mask. I am what I am.'

Sonam was in deep thoughts when her father called. "Hi Dad, I am about to come back. Great! I got into IIM, Lachung. Ya, I know the newly opened IIM in Sikkim." Sonam put down the phone to share the good news with her friends.

When RV hugged Sonam to congratulate her, the hug engulfed them in darkness and sadness. There was an end to this holiday and there was going to be lot of distance – physical distance and the distance that was coming in their dream relationship.

"Now where is this place… Lachung?" Everyone wanted to know.

"This is a small village hamlet in northern Sikkim. From this year, IIM has started a one-year MBA course there," Sonam informed.

"Guys, I will soon be sending my seven lakhs for our resort. I will join you after one year," Sonam said because she did not want their dream, 'Trucks and trucks of love' to be shelved. She was not sure wether she would be able to join them ever.

"You won't come even during the holidays?" Aditi asked surprised.

"No Aditi, two years is abriged into one, so very busy schedule," Sonam said camouflaging the real reason.

Shiv, Aditi and Veer's parents had also agreed to give them seven lakhs each and were quite supportive of their barn resort.

"Yes, even I will be able to arrange seven lakhs by selling my car which my parents gave me for my birthday, if they don't agree," RV said.

"No no, try a few times… we need their blessings too," Aditi said.

19

Six months had passed since Sonam joined classes in Lachung. The MBA had just started that year, hence was a small establishment. Her hostel was a U-shaped, double storey building. The hostel also sat like some Rhododendron. These flowers grew anywhere they wanted to and had an identity as strong as the Lachen and Lachung rivers that flowed in this town. Identity is never determined by size of the thing. But Sonam could not notice anything. Sonam could only see RV's stunning face in her mind. Sonam sat on her bed cross-legged and looked out of the window at the fog which only made the street visible, but covered most of the mountain. Sonam's tears fell and almost froze on her cheeks as it was so cold. Her sweater shoulder dropped from one side, exposing the truck tatoo. The sound of the young rivers and the naughty waterfall never reached Sonam's ears.

She could hear only RV's reply, "I can spend the rest of my life thinking of this one-and-a-half month." When before coming to Lachung she had told RV, "I can't thank you enough for giving me the most beautiful one-and-a-half months of my life." His sentence kept vibrating in her mind as it kept making her feel guilty for not overlooking the meditation part.

'I loved RV as I never got bored with him. I can't enjoy with him if he changes.' Sonam tried to convince herself with this mental dialogue. 'I love my parents too, but I can't enjoy with them because of their over-indulgence in meditations, aartis, meditation camps, silent fasts, and now RV is also going their way.' The mist started coming in her room while she was busy clearing the mist of her mind. She wanted to get lost in the mist, so she did not get up to close the window.

Sonam put on a jacket with a hood and started walking on the street with Rhododendrons growing along the street. She walked past some shops and was walking towards the rivers. When Sonam saw these violet flowers in the mist, it started her dialogue with god. Then she looked up at the snow-covered mountains, the dark clouds which let out some light of dusk and now she was in conversation with god. Sonam of course loved god. "Best form of worship is to celebrate the life that god has created," this is what Sonam believed in.

"Hello aunty," Sonam stopped at a small inn to have tea. "Wow! This is a wonderful sweater you are making, aunty." Sonam told the lady whom she had become friendly with in these six months.

"See, I am making Rhododendron flower valley design," aunty said showing her a colourful sweater.

"Aunty, can you teach me how to make one too? Please?"

"Of course!" the lady said pouring the tea, and gave it to Sonam.

"Can you teach me how to get a truck design over the sweater," Sonam said feeling better at the mention of the truck. "Aunty, please buy black and yellow wool for me to make the sweater and the truck motif."

"I will get you the wool by tomorrow."

"Ok, bye aunty. I will go walk till the rivers," and she kept down the cup.

Sonam walked till the bridge and stood there looking down at the rivers – Lachen and Lachung. As the bluish greyish light of dusk fell in the rivers, the water shone like diamond was crushed into it.

She felt RV's arms circle her from behind and clasp her thin waist. She felt her cold cheek getting warm as he gently rubbed his cheek over hers. He did not speak; she did not speak. As they started walking over the bridge, she slipped her arm over his waist and realized he had hung a guitar over his shoulder. They climbed down nearer to the river and sat on the bank. They sat giving support of their back to each other as RV started playing the guitar. RV played a very lively tune as she started noticing the beautiful Lachung. She enjoyed the music and Rann Vijay Rathore. This was the first time in six months that she enjoyed with RV like she used to during the holiday. It was dark now and lightning slashed the sky into two haves and defeaning sound of thunder made her shudder. Sonam shuddered more when she realized that she was not resting against RV's back but rested against a rock. It was all her imagination.

"I have gone mad," Sonam said it aloud. Sonam got up, thrust her hands in her jacket and started walking back to her hostel. On the way, she checked her WhatsApp for any message from her truck gang friends, specially Rann Vijay. The land for their dream resort had been bought near the lake and construction of the barn had also started. Her friends would keep her updated with the photos of their upcoming resort. But all the excitement of the resort got damped by the occasional photos of meditation shared by RV. He would share them thinking that Sonam will be convinced that he had found a way to control his anger.

"This was the place where we had so much fun washing our truck. And RV is sitting on this rock with eyes closed," Sonam felt disgusted seeing RV's photo.

Aditi's message read – *"We are planning to put RV's photo doing meditation on rocks in our brochure as one of the various things to do at our resort."*

"I don't agree to this." Sonam typed back standing on the street near her hostel.

'This is not the resort of my dream. If people have real fun and happy relations, they would not need anything boring to get into good mental health,' conversing with herself, she reached her hostel room. Lots of assignments were pending and she buried herself into them.

She could only sleep a few hours and now she was climbing the road of half a kilometer slope to reach her department.

Her phone rang. It was RV. "Hi RV, it is little sunny after last night's rain. Ya, I told Aditi. I don't like that idea of your photo doing meditation to be part of our resort brochure. RV, today I have an early morning class. OK bye, will call later." Sonam tried to cut the conversation short.

"Who is RV, Sonam? RV sounds interesting," her friends asked as they walked with her. "RV's full form is Rann Vijay Rathore."

"He is your boy friend?" One of her classmates remarked.

"No, he is a friend. We are five of us – RV, Aditi, Shiv, Veer and me who are working to set up a resort," Sonam replied feeling bad, thinking since when did she started considering RV as just a friend.

They reached their MBA class discussing about the resort. "Wow! This is an awesome concept. We are coming there for the holiday," her friends said. Sonam got busy with her marketing management class after that.

RV held to the phone thinking and got very upset. 'Sonam has stopped liking me. I have not been able to make her understand that I will not get angry like mad. From the time she has gone, we never had a heart to heart talk. We just talk about weather, resort, her studies.' RV kept down the phone and feeling uneasy, he came out in the garden of his Jaipur house. RV's eyes skimmed around the circular lawn. He felt the tents being pegged in his heart when he thought about the night when Sonam was in one of the tents.

Bhagwant Singh came to give breakfast to RV and said, "Sonam bitiya *kaisi hain? Badi pyaari bachchi* hai."

"Bhagwant Singh ji, she is studying in Sikkim. But six months later, she will join us at the resort we are opening in Udaipur," RV replied to Bhagwant Singh but was he trying to reassure himself to shake off his doubts? RV walked on the road circling the lawn when a peacock with huge feathers magestically crossed the road ahead of him. RV stopped as he felt the first impulsive kiss which Sonam had planted on his cheek.

'Oh my god! Sonam always acts on an impulse. Maybe she decided to move away from me acting on her impulse trigerred by my anger,' RV thought. 'If Sonam is busy and couldn't come here in these six months, then I can always go to Lachung. I will tell her how much I love her. I will convince her that I won't become angry like I did.' RV was in deep thoughts when Shiv called.

"Hi Shiv, yes Shiv yes, that blue pottery. Okay, I will message you the address. This is the place where me and Sonam tried our hand on pottery. They will teach you."

RV could see the wheel of their dream resort moving as RV booked the ticket for Bagdogra.

RV drove his hired Innova on the road which sipped the freshness of tea gardens. 'I am sure Sonam is going to say yes.' RV thought as he changed gears and rolled the window down. He increased the speed as he looked at the empty seat besides him, but after a few twists and turns of the hills, he slowed down to reach Sonam safely. The rain which now danced over his windscreen became vigorous. He drove along the mighty Teesta river. The green deep waters, the width, the agility all spoke together one word – power! RV drove along the river gaining strength, confidence in himself and his love, all doubts leaving him. The rain stopped and Rann Vijay stopped by a small tea shop.

RV looked at the diamond-like rain drops evenly distributed over the tiny leaves of the tree under which he was standing. As he took a sip of his tea, he thought, 'If Sonam was here, she would shake the tree' and imagined Sonam's eyelashes stringed with water droplets.

RV was behind the wheel and he put on the heater, as it had started getting really cold now. He had crossed Gangtok, as if the fog lifted his car and placed it on the road to Lachung. He had to still drive for ten hours. 'The mountains looked so magestic. Just looking at them, listening to their heart beat, is actually calming. They have the power to improve a person. The market of the world which is blooming in the name of making people better is all a big lie.' RV thought as he drove through the huge mountains hugged with snow. RV continued with his philosophical dialogue as he took a sharp left turn. The gradient was getting steeper and it was getting colder, but Ram Vijay's heart was getting warmer and warmer as he was nearing Sonam.

"Bhaiya, I want to meet Sonam," RV spoke to the watchman of the hostel while dusting off the flakes of snow from his overcoat. It was nine in the night and warm lights glowed in small shops and hotels. Everything was getting covered with snow and white warm bulb lights looked out of the window, enjoying the snow.

"Sonam is not here," the watchman said warming his hands over a small fireplace in the room.

"Please find out; she must be there. I am coming from Jaipur."

"No, I am certain. The incharge told me she has taken two days permission."

"Do you know where she has gone?" RV said shivering as he realized how cold it was.

"I don't know, but I can call her friend. She would know." The watchman left the room and soon came back with a girl.

"Hi, I am Rann Vijay."

"Yes, I know! You are a part of Sonam's truck gang." Sonam's classmate said as she introduces herself as Miara.

"Where is Sonam?" RV repeated his question, as all his tiredness hit him, making his head spin.

"Sonam has gone to a small village two hours from here. We have seminars with a life coach for two days. Sonam did not want to attend this seminar, so she went off. She will be back after two days," Miara informed.

"Miara, if you can tell me the address of the place she has gone to, I will go there," RV said.

"The village is near Yumtang valley. I am not sure about the name," Miara shifted her gaze from RV to the fireplace in her effort to remember the name. "Yes!" Miara's face glowed as she said, "The owner of the inn down the street knows exactly where she has gone. The lady has arranged for her trip. You go down the street towards the rivers. Name of the inn is Rhododendron. You can also stay there for the night." Miara said with a friendly smile as she was pleased with herself for making things clearer for RV.

"Thanks Miara. You have saved me lot of trouble," RV said while giving her a handshake.

RV's shoes sank into the snow as he walked towards the inn. Rann Vijay opened the door to a very homely ambience. A very fair, pleasant looking plump lady sat by the fireplace, knitting a sweater.

"Hello ma'am. I am Rann Vijay, Sonam's friend," RV said as he took off his overcoat and hung it on the hook near the door.

"You have come to meet her and she is not there," the lady paused her knitting to look at RV.

"Yes ma'am, and Sonam's friend told me you know where she has gone."

"Yes, I have only arranged for her trip. Come, sit near the fireplace; you must be freezing. Have this special winter tea," she said and poured hot tea in a cup from a flask.

"She has gone to see my sister's house in a pasture on the way to Yumthang valley and will stay with my sister there. She should be back tomorrow evening," Aunty said adding more logs of wood to the fire.

RV enjoyed the tea and fire more as he knew that he could go meet Sonam now. "Ma'am, tell me the address; I will go right away." RV stood dusting his overcoat to wear it again.

"It is already eleven and you have already seen the terrain and the weather; you can't go now. Go tomorrow morning. All rooms at my hotel are free, take a room and rest," the lady said, picking up the room keys for him.

"Maybe I can try going now?" RV dialled Sonam's number.

"No use trying the phone or the way; both are unreachable." The lady smiled looking at his desperate condition. RV tried to open the main door of the inn but was able to push only a little against almost half a feet of snow fallen outside. A strong gust of wind pushed the door back and pressed hard against RV's heart.

"Ma'am, you were right. I can't go now."

"Call me Bhutia aunty, that's what Sonam also says."

"Ok, good night Bhutia aunty." The tiredness of the journey saw to it that RV slept till ten in the morning. RV jumped out of the bed to check the weather.

"Oh damn, it is still snowing!" RV said as he looked out. He saw everything covered in thick snow and the buildings, houses stood wearing a thick monkey cap of snow with only their eyes visible. RV felt a little better when he entered the living room of the inn, which smelt of cheese grilled sandwiches.

"Don't get hassled by the snow outside." Bhutia aunty smiled through her extra red cheeks too. "First have hot breakfast," she completed as she set a cute round table not very far from the fireplace, which glowed with its fresh breakfast of logs.

"Bhutia aunty, it has not stopped snowing; would they be clearing the roads?"

"I can understand love is impatient," Aunty said as she settled on the chair next to RV while he gave her a surprised look. "You love Sonam a lot, don't you?"

"How do you know"?

"I also know Sonam loves you a lot too." Now RV was too carried away by the statement and did not ask anything but aunty choose to answer his question.

"Why else would she learn knitting from me and has made a sweater for you? The moment you asked about Sonam, I knew the sweater was for you, because she had asked me measurements for your kind of handsome boy."

RV forgot to chew his breakfast feeling overwhelmed with Sonam's gesture and his love for her swelled in his eyes as tears.

"And she made a very unusual motif on it – a Tata truck.

"Yes that is our special truck. In fact, it is like the sixth member of our truck gang."

"Yes, she told me something about how you planned the truck trip and the summer job. Her face would glow telling me about it. But she would generally feel sad after telling me. Maybe she missed you and everyone else here."

Aunty got up to keep the utensils in the kitchen. "Why did she feel sad when she knew we will always be together when we makes a living with our Truck at the resort," RV wondered, getting a a few lines of worry on his forehead, and many folds of doubt in his heart.

"Where are you going now?" Aunty said when she came out of the kitchen and saw RV all dressed to go out.

"I will try going even if it means going by foot."

"And end up getting buried in snow?" Aunty completed the sentence. "Give me your overcoat and sit by the fireplace. I am your grandmother's age; you should listen to me. You can also spend time, learning knitting like I taught Sonam. Guys can also learn," Bhutia aunty said smiling.

RV sat on the sofa, compelled by her affection. "No one will be able to come in this weather so I am all free to teach you." Aunty picked up her knitting needles and sat next to him. "See, wind the thread around your finger and put on this needle and then take out from the other needle… like this."

"This is amazing aunty, and really requires some skill."

"You try now." Aunty handed over the needles to RV, feeling happy that she was able to calm the young man's mind to some extent.

"I don't understand why did Sonam go in this cold when there was a seminar with a life coach at their institute?" RV said taking out a loop of wool with the needle.

"Why would she be interested to listen to a life coach? She is such a fun girl that life coaches need to take lessons from her," she said taking back the kinitting needles to see what RV has knit.

"I don't think I know Sonam." RV thought and felt so small thinking that how come he missed such an important aspect of the girl he loved so much. This does happen at times, but it does not mean RV loved Sonam any less.

"I suggested some place, a retreat where they do meditation; eat some boiled stuff, litening to silence... all in the name of detoxification, when she asked me where she could go for two days. But she got angry with me. She said, 'Aunty, you haven't understood me in these six months. I hate such places. People talk of connecting with their inner self with the aid of meditation, gurus... But if you are true to your relations, you will never loose contact with your real self.' I was surprised to listen to such truth from a young girl, the truth which very a few people know," Aunty said as she attached a new wool ball to the previous finished one.

"I messed up everything, Aunty," RV said cupping his head between his hands.

"How could you think of anything else? Her smile would have been enough to cure your anger," Aunty said after RV told her all about his visits to meditation camp. "I think Sonam is drifting away from you as she wanted you to completely depend on her to cure you of whatever problem you might have." Aunty tried to analyse the situation, knowing Sonam quite well by now.

"Absolutely, she is so very right! Why only anger, I can overcome anything with her pure love. I have acted like a fool.

But why is this communication gap? Why didn't she tell me?" RV said in a little desperate tone.

"Maybe she thought you would change to impress her but again resort to such things later in life."

"This is exactly the reason as not saying a thing there and then as she feels is not like Sonam." RV said beginning to understand everything.

"Sonam would feel suffocated if her love for life, music dance, fun, hungama was punctured in any way," Aunty said while keeping the needles in her hand without actually knitting and feeling deeply about the situation RV and Sonam were in. The snow kept falling outside, without any noise, making all roads around inaccessible. Silence can be very dangerous. When people don't clear misunderstandings, it creates poison. Relations commit suicide with this poison.

"There is still time, nothing has gone wrong. You can clear all the misunderstanding now," Bhutia aunty said smiling at RV, who was looking into the fire and igniting all kinds of sentences and ideas he would use to clear the misunderstanding. Aunty's soothing voice and positive words induced a new hope in Rann Vijay. He got up and added a few logs of wood to the burning fire.

A faint light of the sun penetrated the window to come inside the room. "RV, the weather is clearing out," Aunty said when she saw the light. RV got up to immediately open the window. He took his head out of the window, tilting his face up, looking at the light which forced its way through the clouds and through thick fog. The effort of the ray did bring a smile onto RV's lips. RV saw some workers hurrying towards the river side, holding snow shovel, rakes, etc.

"Brother, has the way to Yumthang opened?" RV asked.

"No, no. In fact, a huge landslide has been caused by the snow. We are going there," the workers replied.

"Wait, I will also come to help clear the way," RV said.

"No, I don't think you are used to working in these conditions,"one of the workers replied.

"Nevermind. I can be of some use and I disperately need to go to Yumthang valley."

"That won't be possible soon. It's a very huge landslide; a few people might have also got burried inside." RV felt dizzy when he heard that.

"Here, take your overcoat and this is a scarf that I have knit. It will keep you warm. Wear this and get Sonam back." Aunty looked into RV's eyes as she handed over the things to him. RV hugged aunty and left wth the workers.

Bhutia aunty felt very uneasy hearing about the landslide and started praying in her heart for the safety of the people stuck. She wished RV could meet Sonam soon. Aunty was confident that Sonam was safe at her sister's house. Her sister's house was not far from Lauchung. It was one house in that pasture land and most of the winter time, her sister would stay in Lachung. She was there to check a few things and Sonam had gone to stay in that picture perfect location.

Aunty's phone rang. "Coming coming," she said aloud, pleased to hear her phone ring after a long time. "Thank god you called," aunty said, listening to her sister's voice. "There were no signals for two days. Where is Sonam, give her the phone. What! She left yesterday,?"Aunty's voice spoke of the pain she felt when her sister told her that Sonam had left yesterday in a car.

"I have heard one car has come under the landslide and many vehicles are stuck. Phones are not reachable," Bhutia aunty's sister said before her line snapped.

"Hello hello..." Bhutia aunty kept shouting, tried calling back, but nothing helped. She called up different numbers on her mobile to know what had happened in the landslide, but could not reach any. She felt very restless and went on the street to see if someone was there. The ray of sunlight was now overpowered by the dark clouds and increasing fog.

The street was covered by snow. She saw five-six workers coming with a shovel and she knew they were going there. "Beta, can you wait for five minutes, I also want to come with you," she said.

Soon she was off as her snow boots managed the snow she walked over. A bag hung over her shoulder which contained tea leaves, powdered milk and sugar. Her stove, kerosene and water was carried by the workers. Bhutia aunty was born and brought up in Lachung, so walking on snow was not difficult for her and soon they reached the landslide site.

"Why did you come in this cold, aunty?"

"This is my home RV. I am used to this weather," she replied. "RV, Sonam left from my sister's place yesterday," aunty had to tell RV. Both of them looked at the massive landslide and knew she was trapped somewhere there.

"Don't worry son, have faith in god and your true love. She is safe," aunty told RV while keeping her hand on his shoulder. "Now come, help me set the tea-stall."

She set the stove on an old tree trunk under a tent erected by the administration people. The hot tea and Bhutia aunty's presence fuelled everyone there and the work to clear the road took a brisk pace.

The clouds were heavy and hung low. RV looked at the big rocks, uprooted big trees blocking the road and at the clouds which showed it would start snowing again anytime now. The tears in his eyes stung him and his heart bled thinking Sonam was stuck somewhere all alone. RV just kept working like a team with the labourers so that at least he could cross the landslide on foot and see who all were stuck beyond it and reach Sonam fast. The biggest fear was, what if people had got stuck inside it. No one had any information. The chill, the wind almost froze these thoughts and his brain. The tea glass could only warm the hands for a while and by the time it touched the lips, the tea was just warm.

The voice of the electric saw sounded like the shivering of the weak in the cold. RV climbed over the rock, jumped to a fat tree trunk and then down. RV stood in a hollow with huge rocks all around him. He closed his hand over another and tried to press his shaking hands. The sting of the tears in his eyes became unbearable pain which flowed over his cheeks. He became hysterical. RV held himself with his arms, trying to collect himself.

"Sonam come back, please come back. I will always keep you happy," RV kept saying to himself. RV stood feeling hopeless when he saw a small bird fly out of the gap between two huge boulders.

"I need to get back to the clearing work. I have to reach Sonam fast. Nothing has happened to her," he said this aloud to reassure himself, as he had been brought back to his positive state of mind by the little bird. RV wiped his tears and went back to join the labourers.

Bhutia aunty would check if the phone was reachable, while the tea would boil. 'Sonam beta, where are you?' Bhutia aunty's thoughts were constantly questioning while she made sweet hot tea to help the workers in the task. The sky opened its angry fist for a brief period to let the sky light up with lightning before closing its fist into dark dim light and its temper boomed across the mountains and vibrated with the boulders. Everyone at the landslide site shuddered along with RV with the defeaning sound of the thunder.

Everyone brushed the thought that it would start snowing again aside and continued to work hard. The wind started howling in the mountains. The flame of the stove was also being blown, finding it difficult to concentrate on the boiling tea. RV inserted an iron rod under a boulder and tried to move it away. The boulder looked white in the lightning. As the boulder rolled down the mountain, the sound of the thunder also rolled. RV stood with the rod, looking at the landslide which spread almost one kilometre.

"This will take at least two days to clear," RV was thinking this when the snowfall started. Fifty workers along with RV flicked their hoods over their heads and continued to work with their shovels, pick-axes, etc., as if challenging the snow to dampen their spirits. Earth moving trucks had yet to reach there but were on their way not far from Lachung.

By this time, the whole of Lachung village had come to know about the landslide and all households started to help in whatever way they could. Bhutia aunty's supply of water, milk was continuous and now there were biscuits and cakes too. It was a true Indian spirit. Everyone worked, not letting the snow dampen their spirit and they were quite hopeful that earth moving trucks would soon join them.

The snowfall increased almost taking the form of blizzard. As RV stood to take a brief break, he saw through the mist someone in a heavy overcoat and snow shoes talking to Bhutia aunty. RV saw Bhutia aunty's expression go grim. RV felt his heart jump out of his body. His feet froze and refused to walk up to aunty to find out what was wrong. The person turned towards him and he recognized her.

She was Miara. 'What is Miara telling aunty?' RV thought as he felt how it feels when a person is about to faint. His blood drained out of this face, made it look the colour of the snow. When he saw Miara walk towards him, he felt his blood drain out from the rest of his body too.

"RV, there is terrible news," Miara told him as he wished god would take away his hearing power before burying him inside the landslide. "There is another bad landslide a few kilometres short of Lachung," Miara continued.

"What! A landslide? You are saying another landslide had happened?" RV said it aloud to make himself believe it.

"Yes RV, that is exactly what I am saying. The earth moving trucks will not be able to reach on time. But our college students have gone to help the workers there to clear the landslide."

"Great Miara, I am sure you all will clear the area and send us the trucks soon."

"Yes of course, and the slide is not as big as this one."

"Thank god," RV said, pleased that god had not listened to his plea of taking his hearing power.

"Don't worry RV, Sonam is safe. Sonam's zest for life cannot be suppressed by any fall or landslide. She must be keeping everyone's spirit high, even stuck there." RV smiled more as an admiration of his girl than as a reply. "She is a darling of our batch. I had called Bhutia aunty as I was worried about Sonam after I came to know about the landslide. All of us are so worried after she told us Sonam is stuck," Miara said, her face expression turning as dark as the clouds above. "OK RV, all the best. I will go to the other landslide place and help there." Miara left as the occasional opening and closing of nature's fist letting out lightening continued.

Using a rod as a lever, RV threw a big boulder down the slope and thunder boomed as if angry at RV for throwing the boulder down. Everyone at the site came to know that the earth moving trucks would be delayed. They were initially heartbroken, but continued to work harder.

"RV, come sit here. Take a break," Bhutia aunty called out.

RV sat on a rock by a small fire left by the workers who had lit the fire to warm themselves before going back to work. The snowfall had stopped an hour back and the workers managed some dry wood to light the fire and were taking turns to warm themselves. RV sat alone when he felt the fire was not strong enough. He put a biscuit in his mouth and holding it between his teeth, he bent to add some more wood. It was twilight, almost getting dressed for the night.

As RV thrust a log in the fire, he felt someone holding his biscuit with their lips, as he had felt a slight brush of lips. He knew the lips were Sonam's. Without moving, he just turned his eyes to meet hers. He could clearly see her face in the glow of fire, which had a strong presence, as it was all dark now.

Half of the biscuit fell down on the ground as it had got soggy with RV's saliva and RV lost Sonam's image. RV looked at the fire, which now looked blured through the tears in his eyes. More tears kept falling. RV held his head between his palms and with great difficulty, swallowed the half biscuit. RV shuddered when lightning fell on his eyes.

RV opened his eyes which were shut by the blinding light. When he opened his eyes, he saw that flood lights were on to continue the work in the night. The lights flooded him with positivity and he was determined to turn into reality what he had just dreamt. There was no night here. No one slept. Everyone there worked with the flood lights on as they knew there was no day for the people who were stuck in the landslide.

After working for more than fifteen hours, the landslide still looked gigantic, but the will to clear the landslide was even more gigantic. The tedious working in the night flowed into dawn. The flood lights were turned off. The sunlight was let out by the clouds on the condition that it would make the day gloomy. The weak sunlight had no choice but to surrender to the dictum of the mighty clouds. The clouds wanted to have a greater command and they started to shower more snow. RV's face turned grim and pale looking at the snowfall through his lifeless eyes. Wind blew a few specks of snow on his wrinkled purple lips. Now RV's patience had given way. He heard a deafening sound of thunder and this time his anger also vibrated along with the boulders. RV kicked the big bounder in front of him. He didn't feel any pain as the foot was numb with the cold and his senses with the anger. His helplessness was turning into anger. But has any man been able to stand against nature? RV stopped working as his whole body was working for the anger. What a waste! When energy could be used to do something constructive, it was being used for a negative horrible thing – anger. Anger has always burnt its master and never got anything constructive done.

"I can't waste time getting angry," RV thought as the anger was on its way to become wild. "I will never get angry once Sonam is back with me." RV started this self talk and felt himself sitting on the crown of the truck with Sonam by his side, feeling the warm Rajasthan breeze of May. He could feel the warm hot breeze take away his anger and a bit of cold too. He could feel his wrinkled lips smoothening out and a smile slipping over them.

Sonam had finally done it to him. "I had been a fool. Sonam's presence in my life will make me overcome anything. She is my strength." RV's thoughts were halted by some noise. When he looked at the far end of the road, he could see four earth moving trucks. His smile spread like satin on his dry cut lips. The workers jumped in joy on seeing the trucks. Bhutia aunty could feel her tears of joy.

The trucks had cleared quite a lot by evening. Everyone was relieved that no vehicle or person was under the debris. Everyone prayed in the heart for the safety of the people who might have got stuck. Flood lights were on and the work went on briskly the whole night. The sunlight also worked on its strength the whole night and was able to weaken the clouds a bit and came out pale, but not gloomy.

"There is one white Innova," the driver of the truck called out. RV ran over the mud and jumped the rocks with a few people behind him. There were some rocks and lot of mud over it, but it did not look dented by any heavy rock at the first look. There was another huge land mass almost touching the back of the innova. There was no one outside and no movement inside. RV was battling his fears seeing happy lively face of Sonam and gaining strength out of it.

"Sonam! RV shouted and the boulders thought it was thunder again. She was all alone in the drivers' seat. RV pulled the door open.

"Sonam, everything is okay now, don't worry," RV said as he hugged her. Sonam didn't say anything. She just barely kept her arm on his shoulder, when RV felt her arm falling down. She was unconscious. RV checked her pulse. It was there. He scooped her out of the vehicle and ran back over the uneven area.

Aunty had also managed to come some distance over the debris. "Aunty quick, we need to reach hospital," RV shouted.

"RV, get her here fast." Miara was there in her car and had come with some of her classmates from the other landslide site. There was no hospital, but a doctor who treated from his house. He had oxygen cylinders, glucose and the required things and had the most essential thing – sincerity to his profession.

"There is nothing to worry. She is unconscious because of trauma, hunger and thirst. She should be back to her senses by night," the doctor said. Aunty, Miara and her classmates were all there with RV. "It is a miracle she escaped, caught between two landslides," the doctor said

"Doctor, she is a live wire, she is life, nothing can blow her out and she is loved." Miara smiled at RV and then looked at everyone else and said, "by all." Aunty lovingly moved her hand over her forehead, over her hair. The doctor went in the other room where some more people had been brought from the landslide; luckily all were safe.

RV just sat on the stool looking at her when only he and aunty were in the room. "I want to make it very special when she gets up. I want to say 'I love you' in a way she would love it." RV thought about it. "But how?" he questioned in his mind. "It has to be something very special." RV got up almost saying it aloud.

"Aunty, you are staying here. I will be back by evening."

"Where are you going?" aunty asked quite surprised by RV's behaviour.

"I am planning an awesome surprise for Sonam," RV replied.

RV stood at a glass lamp shop which was not so difficult to find in a small bazaar and as the electricity snapped many times during storms. Different types of lamps were there at the shop. RV didn't take time to choose plain glass lamps with a handle to hold on top and a fat candle to sit inside. He took a few metre of thin wire and forty-seven lanterns, and of course, forty seven fat candles. With two big boxes in his hand and innumerable dreams in his heart, he started to walk back.

He reached the doctor's clinic, but didn't go inside. "Sonam is on the first floor and this tree across the road is perfect." RV did some mental calculation and went near a tree exactly opposite to Sonam's room across the road. The tree was all barren, shivering in the cold. RV decided to dress it up, give it some warmth and dress his life too with warmth. RV inserted the wire in the handle and hung it down from one of the branches. Another one stopped a little above it. He hung four candles one above the other to make an 'I'. Then by adjusting the lengths of the wire, he wrote 'I love you'. The fat candles glowed in the safety of the glass lamps dressing up the tree in an amazing way with snow everywhere. The snow all around made the candles look warmer, more so because they were saying 'I love you'. RV admired it before going back to Sonam.

"Now I am leaving you alone with Sonam. God bless both of you," Aunty said before she left for the inn. RV sat watching her face, her lips coming back to their original colour. It was all dark outside, only the lamps reflected the snow around them. RV saw Sonam's lips part slowly as she called his name.

"Yes Sonam, you are fine." Sonam opened her amber eyes.

"RV…" Sonam was going to say something when he put his finger on her lips and guided her to the window with an arm around her. Sonam could feel the warmth of the candles and the confession of love that she had been craving for. RV's love flickered in the candles and her heart too. She rested her head on his chest as she watched, feeling secure in RV's arms circled around her.

"RV, will you always stay like this, till we grow old?"

"No one can be any other way if he gets a life with you," RV said. "I was a fool to have not understood this before. You are like these beautiful glass lamps. I didn't want to spoit them with the soot of my anger. I tried meditation and everything to curb my anger."

"My presence wasn't enough to help you curb your anger?" Sonam asked.

"That was my fault. I should never need any other solace to sort out anything with you by my side."

"But Sonam, why didn't you try to clear the misunderstanding. You just started drifting away."

"May be you would have put up a mask which would wash later in life and I want to live life to the fullest and can't think of being with a person who would resort to stuff I find boring."

"So you acted on an impulse," RV said.

"Yes, you enjoyed my first impulsive kiss, now this was also an impulse. Yes, I always loved you and I found it very painful to see the person I loved change," Sonam said.

"Today, I will give you my promised autograph." She took out a pen from RV's shirt pocket and wrote. 'I love you. You are my rockstar' on his hand. "I love you RV," she said and their lips met when their souls had already met.

"Don't stand for so long. Rest now," RV said cupping her face after a short passionate kiss.

"But RV, I want to see these candles saying, 'I love you' for a long time."

"Okay then come here and lean against me." RV circled his arms from behind and she leaned on his strong chest. They together watched the candles – the warmth of the words – I love you, the warmth of having each other.

20

"Trucks and trucks of love," written in orange on both sides of the truck spoke to the evening. Shiv, Veer, RV and Aditi were all busy setting the mattresses, musical instruments and cushions... inside the truck.

"Hurry up Veer! Put some more fairy lights. Sonam's flight is about to land," Aditi said, seeing her watch.

"RV, you stay here with our truck. We will go inside the airport and get her. You met her in winters. We are meeting her after a year," Shiv said.

"Shiv is right," Veer and Aditi said together.

The three of them left RV there before he could say anything. He leaned against the truck. The orangish rays of the sun flirted with RV's hazel eyes. The rays simmered over his hair which fell in light waves over his forehead. His eyes rested at the gate of Udaipur airport, waiting for Sonam.

Sonam left her trolly to run and hug her friends. "Can't tell you how much I missed you guys." Everyone's eyes were moist with emotions.

"Our live wire is back," Shiv said.

"And never to go back," Aditi added.

"Our live wire was causing quite a stir in Lachung – landslide and all," Shiv joked.

"Yes! I winked at the mountains and they fell for me," Sonam replied back. Everyone laughed together after a long time.

"You scared us to hell," Veer said.

"But good we came to know after it was all over, thanks to the bad network," Aditi said.

"Sonam, RV stayed back at the resort as we are expecting some guests from England," Shiv said, supressing his smile.

"Veer, you go and get the taxi," Aditi said.

They were out of the airport now. "I think we will get a taxi outside the main gate," Shiv said. They spoke non-stop as they had so much to tell each other.

Sonam saw RV and the truck. She gave out a loud shriek of joy and sound of high-fives vibrated with the old priceless memories.

"Welcome Sonam, to the place where you belong," RV said as he extended his hand for Sonam to climb on to the truck. All of them were happy and excited that they all had climbed on to the crown of the truck, stood there making a strong link, holding each other.

Their faces glowed with the happiness. The beginning of their dream life. "Now who is going down and driving?" Aditi said while everyone was in no mood to move.

"Veer, you drive. I want to sit here," Shiv said

"It is sixty kilometres from here. Three of us will drive 20 km each," RV said. Everyone was in a mood to sit with each other at the crown of the truck, feeling the warm summer breeze.

"OK, I go drive first," Shiv said. Sonam pulled a guitar up and started playing a tune. They played the guitar, sang just for the sake of joy without being judged. By the time they reached their barn resort, it was dark.

They entered the resort gate and Sonam could see all the plans they had made on the chart paper, stand in front of her eyes, in real. The head of the barn glowed with 'Trucks and Trucks of Love' written in white fairy lights. The huge windows spilled the light out, making the barn feel one with the fields around. Sonam started her twist of joy. Aditi also started a wild dance. Shiv started playing the drums. Veer started playing maracas, while RV played the guitar. They made their life a rocking party.